MULK RAJ ANAND (1905-2004) was born in Peshawar (now in Pakistan), and educated at the Universities of Punjab and London. He began his career by writing for T. S. Eliot's *Criterion* and went on to win international fame with his heart-warming portraits of the Indian landscape and its people. With a sensitiveness which is uniquely tender and an imaginative fervour which is contagious, his stories and novels explore little known and not-so-familiar corners of the Indian soul and show the technical virtuosity of a master story-teller.

Author of more than a dozen novels, short stories, and critical writings, Mulk Raj Anand was honoured with Sahitya Akademi Award, the most prestigious and coveted Indian award for literary writing, in 1972. He held the Tagore Chair at the Punjab University and has edited *Marg,* a reputed quarterly devoted to the arts. Recipient of several honorary doctorates and other distinctions, he spent the last years at his picturesque retreat in Khandala, a hill station in the Western Ghats outsite Mumbai.

'Mulk Raj Anand's historic importance has already been established... he stands out as a figure of towering humanity whose words guide us through the multitudinous complexity of India with more verve than any other prose writer of his time.'

Alistair Niven in *The Hindu*

By the same author

The Hindu View of Art

The Lost Child & Other Stories

Untouchable

Coolie

Two Leaves and a Bud

The Village

Across the Black Waters

The Sword and the Sickle

Apology for Heroism

The Big Heart

Seven Summers

Private Life of an Indian Prince

The Old Woman and the Cow / Gauri

Conversations in Bloomsbury

Lajwanti & Other Stories

Morning Face

Confession of a Lover

The Bubble

The Mulk Raj Anand Omnibus

A Pair of Mustachios & Other Stories

Man Whose Name Did Not Appear in the Census & Other Stories

Things Have a Way of Working Out & Other Stories

Selected Short Stories (Penguin)

MULK RAJ ANAND

Two Short Novels

Lament on the Death of a Master of Arts
Death of a Hero

Anniversary Commemorative Volume

Introduction by
K.D. Verma
Prof., Univ. of Pittsburgh-Johnstown, U.S.A.

Orient Publishing
DELHI | MUMBAI | HYDERABAD

www.orientpublishing.com

ISBN : 978-81-222-0515-2

1st Published 2012

Two Short Novels: Lament on the Death of a Master of Arts & Death of a Hero

Cover Design by Vision Studio

Published by
Orient Publishing
(A division of Vision Books Pvt. Ltd.)
5A/8 Ansari Road, New Delhi-110 002

Printed in India at
Saurabh Printers Pvt. Ltd., Noida

Cover Printed at
Ravindra Printing Press, Delhi-110 006

Introduction

Saros Cowasjee's laudatory proposal to bring forth a commemorative volume of Mulk Raj Anand's two short novels, *Lament on the Death of a Master of Arts* and *Death of a Hero,* on his birthday will undoubtedly help readers to get acquainted with another challenging side of the celebrated author of *Untouchable* and *Coolie*. While *Lament on the Death of a Master of Arts*, first published in 1938, takes us back to the British colonial India of the modernist era of the thirties, *Death of a Hero* brings us face to face with the historical realities of the beginnings of free India. Evidently, *Lament* is a poetic dirge on the philosophies of pain, loss and grief, but *Death* as an epitaph is Anand's poetic aside on liberty and the function of the poet as reformer and legislator. Undoubtedly, *Lament* could be read as a prose poem on the death of Nur, but in that sense *Death* is also a poetic treatise on the unfortunate death of poet-teacher Maqbool Sherwani. Both these short novels have strong cathartic stratifications that direct the respective heroes to explore the psychological processes of imploding the realities of inner consciousness. Nur's death in *Lament* is a tragic loss perpetrated by the vitiated structure of society, but Sherwani's death is a political murder and hence a sacrificial death. Yet it must be noted that despite some of the obvious similarities, the two novels are distinctly different in style, setting and meaning.

The story of Nur's education, illness and death unfolds a psychosociological process of cathexis and transference, but the story of Maqbool Sherwani is based on direct and fearless action inspired by poetic, moral and political idealism. Yet both the deaths are gruesome and unceremonial crucifixions. Arguably, the two stories must be placed in the larger context of Anand's ideals of humanism, the world of values and the dignity of fellow man as sharply pronounced in the 1945 Postscript appended to *Apology for Heroism.* It is important to understand that Anand's humanism, based on the world of values, is directly focused on the truth of the human condition and that this truth constitutes the basis of the moral and spiritual nature of man's imagination. In examining such intricate issues as human suffering, human dignity and human values in general, how must one rationalize Nur's lost dignity and Maqbool Sherwani's blatant murder? Can Nur ever regain his lost dignity, or must he embrace death as the only recourse? Tragically, for both Nur and Sherwani, the phenomenon of death becomes not only the phenomenon of enlightenment of the difference between the moral and immoral structures of human values, but also the justification of a spiritual interjection of pity.

Ironically, Anand's picture of the British colonial-imperial India of the thirties in *Lament* presents a diseased social order where the function of education, apparently after the Macaulayan system of education, has been constricted to producing *babus,* where family structures are based not on love, compassion and understanding but on the false notions of prestige (*izzat*) and selfishness, and where community seems to lack the basic sense of human values. It is not surprising that Nur, in order to become a *babu,* 'a deputy collector sahib,' must get the degree of Master of Arts. But the M. A. degree does not help him to obtain any high-ranking position, for he belongs to a lower class in the social hierarchy. As a confectioner's son, he cannot compete with other students from upper-class wealthy families. It is rather unfortunate that he cannot take any menial job to feed his family. Now that he is suffering from tuberculosis and is confined to bed, he wants to die. Hence, the famous first line from his own poem, 'Why did you drag me into the dust by making me an M. A.,' a line that constitutes the thematic centre of Nur's tragedy. His painful poetic realization that his education finally led to his tragic failure in life is only a partial realization of the whole process of dehumanization that apparently has been unavoidable to prevent. But who is responsible for this ineluctability? It is Gama's role as a dramatic functionary that helps Nur in the psychological process of reminiscing almost unreservedly. In fact, this psychological process of delving into his own consciousness and hence of unburdening himself of the unforgivable weight proves to be cathartic. His education had prepared him only for the position of a subordinate pillar of the colonial regime of the periphery, but it did not nurture his creative imagination, his poetic vision. Hence, the interjectionist reference to Azad's education, his vision of India and his influence on Nur: 'He initiated me into the mysteries of poetry... The passion, for instance, he put into the reading of books... the slow gradation of Heine's love poems... the lyrics of Goethe and Iqbal... the broad histrionic gesture of Mercutio in *Romeo and Juliet*... the comic overtones of Dickens and the polished undertones of Flaubert...' Nur assures Gama 'that we felt we knew what was wrong with India and with ourselves....' One wonders if the problem with India as identified by Nur and Azad is its subjugation and hence the lack of proper education of its citizens.

Nur is quick to identify the vulgarity and unfairness of the social structure: 'The whole world is in search of happiness... it is vulgar and stupid, the way in which society distributes her favours. The bitch has no morals. She yields herself to the embraces of any robber....' Surely, this is Anand's fierce and bold indictment of the structure of social values, one that denies equality, liberty and justice to its people. It is even more painful to see Nur's continued suffering at home. His father, the Chaudhri, is the most arrogant, heartless and abusive person whose wrongful and cruel expectations of his son have finally driven him to a fateful death. The Chaudhri's frequent rage forces him to imprecate his son: 'Go to hell and be done with it, die and rid us all of this responsibility.' One wonders if Chaudhri's vituperative language is a complicated integument of something more tangible in the relationship between father and son. Nur's mother had died sometime back and his father had remarried. The only sources of some comfort to Nur are his wife, his daughter and grandmother. Ironically, Iqbal came into the Chaudhri household as Nur's wife in a negotiated marriage, but she has been sent back to her parents. Apparently, there is no solution to Nur's suffering. Ultimately, death intercedes and delivers Nur from the wretchedness of his existence. But Nur had been able to penetrate into his inner consciousness in order to see the reality of his existence. The function of Gama and the lucid reference to Azad proves to be an indispensable revelatory technique for Nur to experience what had so far remained essentially hidden in his consciousness. Now that he has seen the truth with this release, he can die peacefully.

While Nur's death in *Lament* provides him cathartic relief, Maqbool Sherwani's death, tragic as it is, becomes a testing point of the protagonist's poetic idealism. It is true that Sherwani returns to Baramula to persuade his friends to endorse the cause of liberty of the Kashmiri people and to oppose the Pakistani intruders. Here, one wonders if Sherwani, the poet-teacher, really understands the truth of his mission. Paradoxically, Sherwani finds himself trapped in a direct confrontation between the world of reality and the world of idealism. His embarrassing discovery that most of his friends in

Baramula have already crossed over to the Pakistani invaders and are in fact trying to force him to follow them leaves him nonplussed. It is here that one finds Anand's mastery in portraying the realism and the truth of the human condition. Although Sherwani finally gets caught and is punished and murdered by his captors, he does not submit to their demands. Nor does he compromise with his idealism. It is indeed very true that his imprisonment by his captors does not weaken his idealism. On the contrary, his commitment to the cause of liberty becomes stronger. Riemenschneider rightly admires Anand's effort and strategy: '*Death of a Hero*, indeed, is not only the deepest probe into the potentiality of man but also most satisfying artistic achievement.' Sherwani's death becomes a messianic sacrifice and hence the emblematic triumph of the human values that constitute the very core of Anand's humanism. Sherwani's letter to his sister that he wrote during his imprisonment simultaneously marks the triumph and also the continuity of the impact of art on civilization.

In the Postscript to *Apology*, Anand has raised the question of the inveterate need to know the truth of the human condition and the human values that strengthen the human condition. In this search, then, can the human imagination eradicate the problems of human suffering, pain and subjugation and can humanity at large seriously consider *karuna* (pity) an interjectionist alternative and a fundamental and integral human value? 'The Buddhist *Karuna*, or compassion,' explains Anand, 'which is neither contempt from above, nor sentimental love from below, but a tender recognition of the essential similarity, both in strength and frailty, of human beings, becomes for me the pervasive starting point of comprehension for each feeling, wish, thought and art that constitutes the world behind the scene of the human drama, from which catharsis of ultimate pity may arise.' Interestingly, in his letter to his sister,

Sherwani maintains that pity is dependent on one's conscience and that when fully realized, 'pity is poetry and poetry is pity.'

University of Pittsburgh–Johnstown, U.S.A. K. D. Verma
2011

Lament on the Death of a Master of Arts

Dedicated to Marian Evans

Lament on the Death of a Master of Arts

'*Ohe,* what is your condition?' Nur heard the voice of his father through his broken half-sleep as from faraway. His eyes opened against his will. In the stillness of that hour the gigantic, padded-faced, wry-mouthed presence of the Chaudhri, terrifying like Nero, seemed inauspicious. Nur closed his eyes, dipping them into the comfort of sleep and escaping from the fear that his father's form sent through him...

'*Ohe,* what is your condition? I am asking you,' said the Chaudhri advancing from the foot of the bed. And, without waiting for an answer, he continued: 'Have you been comfortable in the night? You haven't had any blood, I hope?'

Nur was terrified that his father would come nearer. Half opening his eyes, he said in a whisper: 'Better.' And, as if to ward off the Chaudhri's stare, he tried to assume the casual tones of the healthy person which he knew he was expected to be.

'Why can't you answer properly, swine? Why do you sulk all the time?' the Chaudhri said, his grey-green eyes flashing. 'You should try and make an effort to get well, as I can't go on breaking myself to pay the Doctor's fees every morning?'

'I am better, Chaudhri*ji*,' Nur said, still assuming a normal manner. 'I am much better.'

'*Achha* then, wake up now and mention the name of Allah-*mian* for a change,' the Chaudhri said softening. And he hesitated for a moment, looked round the bed and added: 'Your grandmother will be coming down soon...'

Then shaking his head and making a grimace, he swerved on his feet and walked away.

Nur closed his eyes so as not to see his retreating form. A moment before the Chaudhri had turned, the boy's gaze had fallen on the prickly silver bristles of his unshaven beard and he recoiled. He could hear the stamping of the Chaudhri's feet going down the stairs. He quavered, struggling to throw off the spell of fear which his father cast on him. He twisted his lips as waves of resentment warmed his heavy, sleepy limbs. 'No, I don't want to live,' he said with the obstinate spite of a child, and then to strengthen his sense of opposition, added: 'I wish I were dead.' And as soon as he said it he wanted to stifle the thought: his father's footsteps were out of the reach of his ears now.

The body of death lingered on the sick bed, wrapped in a white shroud...

Waking in a hot sweat from his half-sleep he could see it lying there, on the giant bed in the narrow front room on the first floor of his father's congested two-storied house. It was his own body; it looked like a corpse because he had gathered the sheet tight round him at night, and because he was dying, dying of consumption.

A slight tremor of panic ran through him at the thought, with a subtle violence. He stirred on his back and shuffled his legs about. Then, quickly loosening the sheet from his side, as if he were arranging himself in readiness for the visit of the Doctor, he spread the cloth till it sagged into a ruffled disorder, and sought to still the ache of apprehension.

If only his heart would stop fluttering, he thought impatiently. 'You mustn't talk of death,' as grandma would say, 'May I be your sacrifice; and what an inauspicious talk they do.'

He moved his head, but couldn't shake off the vision, so he began to hum the melody of a verse written by Iqbal, his wife's namesake, a favourite tune of his. The half-serious, half-playful sentiment in it was so appropriate.

'Your love has straightened all the curves of my life...'

He didn't complete the verse; the lack of faith in his voice betrayed the fear for his lungs.

He was becoming obsessed again now...

His fine face, with the slightly dilated nostrils, with the brown eyes bulging out of the deep sockets and the indrawn cheeks, was flushed, not with the rich pink of the Sahibs, as it had always been flushed since his childhood, but with the shame of a rose which has withered before it has begun to bloom. His body was limp except for the spine, which ached as it had ached increasingly through having to lie in bed day after day for five months, and the hard ribs and collarbone which seemed to crack as they rose out of his transparent flesh like the dry roots of a bare tree still sound at the heart. But he was calm as if his whole body, eaten through by the germ, was sensitive to his doom; the clear forehead that sighted with cool composure each anxious thought in his fevered brain, wrestling with the problem of how to get well; the skeleton of his chest which rose and fell with the nervous heartbeats beneath it as if eager to know how to get better; the tender eyes that bent their light, now inwards, now outwards, and the dry lips on which the ghost of a sigh waited to become evanescent.

During the past months he had felt his perceptions become acuter: he had noticed the change from summer to autumn in almost every shade of air, as it touched his eyes, his lips, his ears and the cells of his body. But lucidity of this knowledge was being continually baulked by the fear, the obsession which possessed him.

He turned over and felt the terror of falling from the terrace at the top of the house. Only it was like a fall in a slow motion picture, slipping slowly past every fraction of an inch. If only one could catch hold of the projection of the terrace, or if only there was an obstruction on the way, one might be saved. Why didn't the Chaudhri have wooden awnings built on the top of the windows? They would have arrested the glare of the sun during the day, and they would have checked a fall if someone, anyone, a child or, no, a cat fell.

He made an effort to stop the morbid run of his thought, shook his head as if to deafen his own cries and blinked his eyes at the phantom of peril.

'Life is short and art is long,' he muttered tiredly a phrase he had learnt at college. Then he lifted his head and looked at the bars of light which shone like the silvery spokes of the day through the chinks of the closed windows. 'Grandmother will be coming down from the kitchen to see me,' he said to himself.

She always came down first thing in the morning, the poor old woman, and again the last thing at night. And when he was a child, she had told him lots of fairy stories. He remembered that one which she had told him after his mother had died and which he had retold her with several variations during the holidays.

'How did it run?'

~

Once upon a time there was a little boy whose father was a confectioner in the bazaar and whose mother was a beautiful houri. And he had an old grandmother who loved him very much and who used to take him to his father's shop to eat a sweet pancake and semolina every morning. And he used to toddle and walk holding the hand of his father among the grease and the grime, among the soot of steaming cauldrons and deep black-bottomed pans, full of treacle and clarified butter, and the mud of coolies' feet bearing sacks of sugar, fruit and flour. And then he had learnt to speak. And when he spoke it was such a pretty speech that they said to his father: 'He ought to be sent to the Government school when he grows up, for he will surely become a babu with his pretty speech.' And because he had a lovely pink face, with dark brown eyes and sleek brown hair, they said: 'He will surely pass his MA and become a deputy collector sahib.' And he had been so happy to hear their prophecies, and he had become so naughty and enthusiastic, that he would smack anybody who did not give him a pice just as if he were already a deputy collector. But when he was five, the cruel angel Izrael had come and taken away his mother. And he had cried when his mother, who was a houri, did not come back from the heaven where she had gone visiting. And another woman had come into their house instead, who, his father had said, was his new mother. But she was only a little bigger than he and he could not call her mother as she quarrelled with him over the toys when they played together. And he had been sad as he had never been sad before. But his grandmother loved him and doted upon him just like his mother, and she laid him in her arms as she made garlands for sale in the bazaar. And then, one day, his father had come to him and said to him that he was grown up now and must go to school to learn to be a big babu and get an MA pass, and that he would receive a pice a day for his pocket if he did his lessons well, and that if in addition he came home and learnt the Koran and said the five prayers prescribed by religion, he would get two pice. And that was the day he had started to be a 'Master of Arts'.

~

'But, oh, why did they drag me into the dust by making me a Master of Arts?' he wearily protested, falling back exhausted, the words trailing like a long pain though they had emerged quite casually in a spontaneous new rhythm.

There was the glow of revelation about them, about the ordinary but natural and expressive sequence into which they had flowed, even though they were born of the doom which sat on him. And the memories of his past seemed to come back to him in their track as if they were an 'open sesame'; seemed to come back with the force and vivacity of rapiers thrust in the raw wounds of his heart. For from the first cry at birth his life had been pain-marred.

'Sh, sh,' his mother had warned the world and consoled him, the inconsolable: 'What is it' then, 'didums, di, di, mother's darling, di, didi, dum...' then 'he is hungry... don't cry,' then, 'mother's dearest, loveliest darling... he has been neglected' then... 'my pet... my darling... don't cry then...' And she had swayed him in her arms, cheek to cheek, flesh to flesh in tenderness... slow glory of touch crept into the rapture of smiles, bubbling with the joy of being borne and tickled to laughter...

'Oh mother, oh mother, where are you now?'

Beyond the corpse in the darkness of the grave she had become a ghost. In the silence of his doom he wondered whether through the barriers of all these years, her heart could still beat with a piteous sound for him, whether it could still bleed with warm love and anguish at the sound of his tears. 'In the name of the merciful and the compassionate God,' she used to say, and gather him into her arms if he woke up in the night, gather him with a surging agony of warmth, answered only by his cries, and still patient when his father heaped all the curses and all the abuse, all the complaints of the mortal wrongs he had suffered to be awakened by the row... Ebbing with time, receding into thin air, remote she was now, buried under the mound of earth in the cemetery outside Lohgarh gate, which was surrounded by the aura of fear in the night, of suspense in the still whiteness of the noon, except on Fridays when people went to visit the Pir who kept guard on the graves and muttered charms to keep the ghosts away, in return for the gifts and for the pice tendered to him. He remembered the horror of a moment when his grandmother had taken him there and he had seen a skull beside a crumbling mound in the empty sockets of which millions of ants were crawling. He had wondered whether his mother had become an ugly demon with a malevolent steady stare in the pits of her head and a terrible changeless grin on the thrusted teeth exposed from hard, indrawn lips.

But surely she wasn't eaten by the worms... No, no, not his mother... though why not?

He jerked his body and compressed his lips tight so that he shouldn't moan, shouldn't even sigh, and he took the fingers of his right hand to his left to feel the pulse, though he didn't listen to the verdict, only mechanically registering the pumping of the blood.

Far off from this dawn, remote, half forgotten, ages before now, before the high school and college, there was a queer impatience, in the feel of early mornings, the fear of being late at school, the violent motion in the belly even as he had gulped hot tea and swallowed mouthfuls of fried parathas dipped in mutton gravy... Thank God, one was rid of that, though it had taken him a long time, for he was seldom ill even though he had prayed in secret to be ill... As he had hurried on his way to school, the dizzy vision of the Master's perpendicular rod had blotted out space and time, while the clothes stuck to the flesh in the clammy heat and perspiration of summer mornings. His grandmother had no sense of time and did not start cooking his meal until she had said her prayers and swept the rooms of the house from the top storey to the ground floor... He had begged his father to buy him a watch, one of those nice shiny watches with a chain which he could carry in the pocket of his waistcoat to school, as all the other boys had watches and wouldn't show them to him except from a distance, affecting to be superior Sahibs like Mercado Sahib, the Headmaster. But his father had said, that he ought to get up by the muezzin's call at dawn and say prayers every morning. And then this additional trouble had been added to his difficulties as a kind of reward for his attempt to be happy and fashionable. For, as the fat mullah in the mosque at the end of the narrow lane, in which the flies buzzed over the children's yellow excretions in the drain, sounded the muezzin's call, he had to shake himself out of the bed lest his father might beat him for disobeying. And, although he did not know how to say the prayers, he had to run to the mosque to do the *wuzu*, wash himself, join the congregation and follow it in the various postures: sit, stand, kneel, rub his forehead on the ground and murmur the verses in Arabic which the mullah had taught him by rote during the special lessons he gave him in the evenings, in return for the rich meals, the new turban, the shirt, the shalwar, the shawl, the shoes and other 'presents' which he received for looking after the spiritual welfare of the Chaudhri's son. 'God gives man gifts to obtain his own ends.' He muttered the proverb ironically.

What was the use of all those prayers, he had never been able to discover in his life. He had never been able to learn Arabic well enough to understand the Koran, though he had repeated the Suras from the first page to the last hundreds of times. What was the use of cleaning and purifying oneself, for instance, if the clothes one wore when saying prayers were soiled by all the dirt of the streets and the sweat of the body at night... And though he had never told anyone, while he was saying prayers on a constipated belly he had involuntarily discharged a stinking wind which had fairly resounded back from the walls of the mosque to his own ears, so that it had made him burst out with an embarrassed laugh, though the elders in the congregation who were themselves used to letting loose wind had carried on with their prayers, only turning their eyes a little. He had been afraid that God must have heard it, but then he had reassured himself that since he discharged wind because of the exercise involved in kneeling, bending, standing, sitting and kneeling again, which was the prescribed method of saying prayers, surely God would forgive him for his sin. 'Thus is the word of thy Lord verified against those who commit abomination!' What a fool he had been to grieve over the wrath of that impotent oracle of blind vision, 'the merciful and the compassionate God, to whom all praise belongs, who is the Lord of all worlds, the ruler of the Day of Judgment, whom all humanity serves and whom it asks for aid and to whom the fat mullah calls out in deafening cries every morning, noon, afternoon, evening and night!'

'In the face of the falsehood and lure of the world, I could laugh,' he said to himself.

And yet he felt cheated to be fading away imprisoned in this room with his allotted hours and days, how many he did not know, being conscious only of his heart beating, pounding at his chest in the silence of the morning, mingling with the hum of a long-drawn wail, far off like the din of his soul in strife, and near, as near as where the cock crowed on the roof of someone's house in the gulley.

The illness seemed to have deafened his ears as if the burnt-up tissue in his body had risen in the haze and clogged that sense, but otherwise he felt lighter, more transparent. He applied his ears and listened attentively, his gaze fluttering as though he were looking for something which he had lost in this room or was trying to remember something which he had forgotten.

'*Allah-ho-Akbar*,' came the voice of the mullah.

'*Dur, dur,* dog,' Nur murmured rising out of his resignation, angered by the groans of a dry as dust formalist fed by the food of charity.

'Call the faithful to prayer, call them to prayer, you dog. I hate you and I hate your God. I hate you all! To incur your wrath I spit on your face and I spit on the face of your God!' And he was about to raise himself from his pillow to give his words the confirmation of the act when a choking cough seized him and he was caught in the paroxysms of an agony that seemed as if it would be his last.

'Nur, Nur, my child, what is it my son? What is it, my darling son?' his grandmother called, coming down the stairs.

She had the lines of her seventy odd years written on her face and hobbled miserably, shaking her head as if she were drunk.

He coughed and the effort seemed to stir each fibre of his being, the scourge of that uncertainty which had possessed him for months.

His grandmother bent her twisted, wrinkled face, straining to touch his forehead with her lips, but unable to do so as the salt tide of tears dimmed her sight. Her hands shook convulsively with the effort of bending.

'What is it, my child? What is it, my son? May I be your sacrifice!' she soothed with pouting lips.

'Nothing, grandmother, nothing is the matter,' he said gasping for breath as if he had lost a heartbeat. 'I am all right, I am all right. You go and rest.'

'Do have some of the tea I have made for you, my son,' she said, 'do have a sip. . . I will open the windows — the sun is shining outside.' But as he had closed his eyes and paled for a moment, she opened her mouth, frightened and looked at him dazedly.

'*Achha, achha*,' he sighed impatiently lest she should fuss. 'But don't open the windows. You go and rest.'

She hobbled by the side of the bed and relaxed. Then with indifferent fingers she pulled the quilt, which he had thrown away on one side during the night, over his legs. Glancing around to see whether everything was in order she scanned his face casually, as if she had come to accept the deathlessness of his sick body, and she lingered by the bedside.

He felt oppressed by her presence as if she had disturbed him and brought on his spasm of coughing.

'It isn't that I am a child anymore, grandma,' he said. 'I will be all right, you go and rest.'

'You are still a child to me, my son,' she said. 'Are you sure you will be all right? There is your tea. I have put it on the shelf. Now are you sure? I will see to the meal then. I will go.' And looking around and under the bed, she lifted the chamber and said again: '*Achha*, I will go. But call me if you need anything...'

As the image of her hobbling, bent form receded, he pitied and hated her. She was his father's mother. And always he had pitied and hated her. The pride of his love for his dead mother had never overcome the barrier of the wrong she had done him in allowing his father to marry again. And since she had aged too he had never been able to overcome her ugliness; and the weight of her doting affection had only increased the barrier.

In the prolonged weariness of five bedridden months the ebb and flow of his hope in life had infused in him a strange tenderness for everyone and he had loved her for her devotion. She was old and stupid and stumbling, but there was something so pitiable about her that he had let her take the place of his mother. And yet the bitterness of her calm acceptance of his father's brutality persisted, the bitterness of those howls which he had uttered when his father beat him and the tears he had shed, tears of shame and chagrin when he had been made to accept the humiliation of orders from his stepmother, of the suffering they had all tried to extract from him.

'They all tried to oppress me, they have broken and crushed me and left me destroyed, and now they make a fuss of me and fetch me medicines and run here and there trying to save my life, the hypocrites!' he muttered under his breath, and looked away at the books that lay by the bottles of medicine on the narrow shelf, crowded by the odds and ends of his stepmother, her looking glass, and her assortment of glass bangles.

As he turned over he felt the weakness of his lungs go silently to his head, and he lay still in a sleepy inertia through which the bundles of dirty clothes that hung like festoons from the coloured pegs on the walls, the stacks of cheaply painted trunks and the sacks of sugar over which the rats had pissed in stinking green patterns, seemed to become unbearably depressing. The whitewashed walls blackened by the soot of slow hearthfires in the gulley seemed to be crowding in on him and the feeling that he could never get up and escape from the sordid reality of his home into the world of tall mirrors and gilded chairs and mahogany tables depicted at the Mahna Singh Theatre, made him hopeless.

A fresh twitching of the lungs frightened him. He closed his eyes and tried not to move even the fraction of an inch, obsessed by the superstitious awe which the Doctor's orders not to excite himself in anyway had spread over him.

And, for a moment, he lay resigned and apathetic like a corpse which does not care about the soil it is laid on, though his eyelids pressed heavily and his nerves quivered as if his inside had become more acutely sensitive to the fear and sorrow that had crushed him through the last months.

He felt a hard knot of saliva settling in the passage of his throat.

He stirred his throat and half opening his eyes, spat into the spittoon. He closed his eyes, afraid to see the dark-red-white flame trailing down from his mouth. He fell back exhausted. It was terrible to be so weak. He sought to rest again, closing his eyes in the warmth through which swirled the noise of sparrows twittering in the lane. He lent himself to the soothing warmth of the pillows beneath his head and accepted his helplessness.

'What was I thinking before Grandma came?' he asked himself. But there was no answer from the depths of his body which now seemed stretched in a repose morbidly expectant. His heavy heart beatout a refrain; 'I must get well, I must get well,' as if it were still drugged with its obstinate belief in existence. And there was a quickening at the back of his head.

In the dim light of the half-sleep which came over him, beyond the massed clouds of darkness, he was walking by the thick, muddy, sewage stream overflowing with slime, that ran in the shadow of the town's red brick wall and into which people emptied rats, live snakes, dead dogs and cats... There was the foul reek of dung and urine from the trolley train which ran from the houses of the sweepers through the town wall past the gate of Lohgarh to the vast valley near the Bhagtanwallah Gate, where the refuse was burnt... He had often wanted to become an engine driver so that he could drive the little engine of this train... But the vision of the black-skinned, white-clad Master with a primly cut, scraggy beard had remained. The Master stood in the classroom, by the shoemakers' houses, the corners of his eyes shot red with rage as if he were made of some unearthly clay, and he, Nur, had entered late. In one fearful moment he had trembled merely to see the fresh cane which lay on the table; he had known that the accusation in the Master's eyes was coloured by revenge rather than by the anger at his lateness:

the Master had asked him to bring him a basket of sweets from his father's shop and when he had begged his father to give him the gift to offer to the Master, the Chaudhri had refused, saying, 'I don't keep a shop for the purpose of charity, it is hard enough for me to make a living and pay your school fees.' And, of course, he had never dared to tell this to the Master... The dread of the greedy dog, as he stood there, grimly seeped into his bones. And when the demon actually lifted the cane, he began to shriek in agony, whereupon the Master shouted to him, 'Be quiet or I will give you one stripe more for everyone after which you howl!' And as he howled and cried, 'Oh spare me, oh spare me, Masterji,' long before the sweep of every blow from the cane shimmered before his terror-stricken eyes, the ghost of the devil had worked himself up to an even grimmer rage so that his words tumbled over each other as he numbered the blows, while he begged, prayed, supplicated to the cruel tyrant, drifting further and further and shouting the more, though he knew that his protest would increase the sum of his punishment...

In a corner of the room he sat alternately hating his mother, who stood in the chamber of horrors, in the oblivion of her hell raging with fire and water, for not coming to his rescue, and loving her as she stood with tears of despair in her eyes and arms outstretched, appealing to the angel Gabriel to help her son. 'Oh mother, don't be silly; don't whine like a pauper,' he said as he nursed his smarting limbs, unable to lift his eyes for shame, as the tears welled in them against his will. 'We have some prestige. The Chaudhri is respected by the whole bazaar and I shall ask him to report to the Head Master...' But if the Chaudhri saw the Head Master the Munshi would become far more revengeful... Already he had made a slip at spelling and the Master was putting pencils between his fingers and pressing them hard, hard, harder, and Nur could see himself writhing and shrieking and crying as he rolled on the floor to release his cracking bones from the Master's grasp...

The torment flushed his face above the dream which strayed vaguely back from the school compound to the cement tank in which the devout at the mosque washed their feet in muddy water...

He was swaying up and down, reading the Suras aloud by the light of the cotton wick soaked in olive oil in the earthen saucer lamp in a corner of the mosque, the Koran laid on a bookrest before him, when he felt himself dozing from the fatigue of a long day. Suddenly from the darkness behind him there was a kick in his ribs and Maulvi Shahab-Din stood, caressing his beard and shouting: 'Beware, son of a swine, and recite the Suras or else your mean, dirty father will tell me that I don't deserve any new clothes this year because I haven't taught you to remember the Suras...' And coming home through the dark, dirty lane where bulls roamed and fakirs prowled, he slipped into the gutter and bruised his elbow and cried to his grandmother. His father was in the lavatory upstairs and terror seeped into the house. The Chaudhri came down suddenly and gave him two slaps for complaining and whining all the time, and he was sulking with the shame of his humiliation, not showing his face to anyone, refusing to eat his food and abusing grandma, and she was saying she would buy him some sweets at a shop which stock English peppermints.

Now the barren waste of a flat plain arose, rank with cactus and brown burnt grass smouldering in the heat of the day, beyond which loomed a fortress, dirtied by time to an ochre, brown cinnabar, except for the crimson cupolas and battlements overgrown with moss. He was wandering alone in it, making for the moat which was full of stones and splinters and knife-edged grass, and as he drifted across it, sulking and forlorn, he was whimpering in a broken, self-pitying voice: 'Why doesn't God give me death?' The fortress became the formal red brick building of the Government High School and beyond were two mounds like pyramids in the desert of Kerbala; a caravan of camels, tied nose to tail, tail to nose, was travelling slowly in the torrid glare of a blue sky whitening with the hot sighs of the burnt earth and with his sobs, as he ran to and fro, looking for the shade of a palm tree, on bare feet blistering with the fire of the bright yellow sand... He was weeping with broken, spluttering cries, the sweat was pouring down his body, and he was tired of his fruitless search for the oasis in the barren expanse of the sun-soaked land. Now he was on the outskirts of the Railway Station, and by a dump of iron girders, wooden beams, the cinders of burnt coal and rubbish, stood a grove of trees surrounding a tank. He stooped and put his mouth to the pool in the forest like an animal and drank off the liquid till his belly was bursting.

As he turned round to look at the jungle it was Gol Bagh where he had gone to play cricket with his friends during the school days... He was alone and it was twilight and he was hurrying home, afraid that his father would beat him if he had happened to come home from the shop to relieve himself and found that Nur hadn't returned. But not all the alacrity he put into his steps could shorten the long dusty distance to Lohgarh past the fuelwood stalls, past the dirty, greasy cookshops for travellers, compared to which his father's shop was a luxury palace, past the pedlars who hawked cabbages, turnips, cucumbers and melons as they bent over their three-wheeled, square, box-structured wheelbarrows, to guard against the pilfering Hindu women who refused to move without getting something for nothing after they had made their purchases, past the panting Kashmiri coolies, loaded with sacks of flour on their back, their brows glistening with sweat and feet coated with mud, and past the stream of dead Hindus swathed in red cloth painted with golden stars borne hurriedly along for a late funeral by groups of men chanting, 'The name of God is Truth...' The slow chant seemed to become muffled, turning into the whisper of a breeze which was creeping into him with the premonition that one of the ghosts, which according to the Hindus strayed about the earth before rising to heaven, was following him and would pounce on him if he looked back...

Though there were people about, though he had walked far away from the funeral ground enclosed by a high wall where the dead were burnt, he was possessed by the dread, so that he started running fast, heading straight for his father's shop instead of going home under the lonely shadow of the city wall... In the sullen eyes, staring out of the Chaudhri's body was a cruel power. 'Where have you been, rape mother?' and Nur trembled to see the sweat pouring down his father's hot, angry face in the light of the smoking kerosene lamp. 'Where are your shoes, swine? Where have you lost them? Where have you been eating the dust?' the Chaudhri burst out as he caught hold of a rope and came to hit him. 'There is no talk, Chaudhri*ji*, forgive him,' a customer interceded, taking Nur under shelter. Whereupon the Chaudhri swung back to his seat scattering the flies off the foodstuff and cursing: 'What is the use of having a son! He goes about loafing! As if I was a millionaire and he had nothing to do. It wouldn't occur to him to come to help me for a few hours. And now he has lost his shoes! Where did you lose your shoes?' Nur was dumb with terror and began to sob, feeling as if one of the evil ghosts had come and taken possession of his father and would probably follow him home and kill him in the dark of the lane. 'Why don't you speak?' the Chaudhri said and leapt upon him dealing blows till the whole bazaar crowded round to save him from his father's wrath. The customer who had been shielding him had lifted him and brought him home... He was still weeping and didn't want to face anyone, not even his benefactor nor his grandmother. He only wanted to sleep... But there was broad daylight out of the windows and the air didn't seem sinister... What was that?...

He opened his eyes with a start, so suddenly that the pupils under his heavy-eyelids smarted and there was a cracking ache at the back of his head. There stood Gama, a tall black boy who had been a class-fellow of Nur's since the Infant form till he had been left behind in the fifth class through successive failures, and had given up schooling to become a tonga-driver for Fateh Ali, the contractor.

'Still asleep, Nur, childling?' Gama asked. 'How are you now? I was passing this way. I thought I would look in and see you.'

'Come, do sit down,' Nur said in a slow voice. 'I was just dozing, just thinking, half dreaming, curiously enough I was dreaming about our old school.'

'And I opened the windows and let in the sunshine on that purgatory,' Gama said with a mischievous light in his eyes. Then sitting down on an edge of the bed, he bent his head and continued: 'What is there in education, brother? Waste of time.' He was half chagrined as he had never been able to outlive the reproach of having failed in his education, and half-audacious because of a genuine contempt for learning that he had achieved since he had become a tonga-driver.

'Education, education, brother,' said Nur affecting a learned voice, 'education means wisdom; wisdom means the correlation of the growth of body and mind: the correlation of the growth of body and mind is achieved through knowledge and knowledge is power: if you have enough recommendations, that is.' After this he smiled a nervous, apologetic smile as if he were afraid that in spite of his faint mockery, Gama might think he was showing off his superior knowledge, for his friend, in spite of the fact that he was earning more than hundreds of MAs, had a feeling of inferiority engendered by the exaggerated respect for degrees that people had, specially as he was employed in a profession which was well known for its low hooliganism. Seeing, however, that Gama was smiling good humouredly, Nur added: 'You are right, brother. You are right.' And he heaved a deep breath and changed his side as if to shake off his lethargy. Gama's visit had surprised him.

'Do you remember Master Kanshi Ram?' asked Gama, laughing. 'When we were in the fifth primary class...'

Nur smiled in answer. He did remember for he had suffered from Kanshi, who had established a vendetta against him, because he refused to accept the privilege of taking private tuition from the Master, alongwith the sons of the rich merchants of the cloth market. Kanshi charged ten rupees a month from each of the boys and Nur didn't know how he could ask his father for the money, specially as it was well known that the Master made immoral suggestions to the boys when they went to his house to be coached. One day when he had been left alone in the classroom filling his satchel at the end of the school session, Kanshi had even tried to kiss him and because he had refused to be kissed, the Master had beaten him on the knuckles with a ruler the next morning by making the flimsiest excuse about his pronunciation as he read aloud. Nur had told Gama, who had caught hold of Kanshi by the scruff of the neck that very afternoon and threatened to kill him if he didn't behave, after which, indeed, Nur had been safe.

'I often see him about,' Gama said. 'He has got grey hair now but he is incorrigible. He still goes about chasing boys. I regret that I didn't beat him up, the old sod...' There was a slight bravado in his voice and he chuckled to think of his exploits of those days when he was a wild, free creature, respected for his courage, and not the slave harnessed to Sheikh Fateh Ali's tonga, like a skinny horse. Then he bent his head again and seemed to retreat into himself.

'What is the talk?' Nur asked, feeling the slow burning of a fever in his flesh. He turned his side and saw a basket of fruit by his bed which apparently Gama had bought. 'Why did you do that?'

'There is no talk of that, brother,' said Gama. 'You will get well and we won't care for the limp lord. After all, you used to let me copy the sums from your notebooks during the vacations — although do you remember the occasion on which my father almost broke my bones when he caught me copying your answers and I ran away to Calcutta...?' And he laughed.

'Yes, I remember,' Nur said.

It was not so much the memory of Gama's troubles that he recalled, however, as those of his own. But how far away seemed those endless days when he had trudged to and back from school from this house in Dhab Khatikan, through the narrow deep-rutted intricate bazaars, full of puddles of rain water, where the carts got stuck against each other and held up the traffic for hours; days of utter loneliness only relieved by the few hours of play and an occasional fair to which he was taken by his grandmother; when he had been baulked by the terror of *jinns* and *bhuts* and *churels* and other denizens of the nether worlds over which, the Koran said presided His Satanic Majesty, the Devil, days when he had become conscious of the dearth of books and friends and of his father's poverty which was responsible for them, dull, irrelevant days when he was obsessed by the desire to grow up as quickly as possible. He had wanted the dignity of age.

'I have written, rather thought of, the first line of a poem this morning,' Nur said.

'Who is there? Who is that with you?' came the voice of his grandmother from the top of the stairs. 'It is not your father, is it?'

'No, grandma...' he called back.

'It's me, Gama, grandmother,' the visitor shouted so that Nur might not strain himself by answering, and he turned to his sick friend to see if he had been disturbed by his shout.

Nur's face was glowing with a pale light though there was a distant look in his eyes, as if he was excited by the visit of his friend, and yet beyond caring for company. So few of his old college friends came to see him, that his whole body seemed thrilled by this contact.

'Are you sure that I am not tiring you?' said Gama. Nur moved his head in negation and smiled.

'*Achha* then, what is this that you have written, my poet?' asked Gama half-mockingly.

'I offer the beginning,' Nur said, affecting the elaborate manner of Urdu poets.

> 'Why did you drag me into the dust by making me an
> M.A...'

And then, half closing his eyes, he sought to control the muscles of his mouth which were weakening. But he was overcome by self-pity and he felt the tears come to his eyes. He tried to show a brave face by grinding his teeth as if he were swallowing some poisonous physic which was soon going to twist his body into an ugly horror.

Gama sat still for a moment, looking away, then he leant on the bed and laid a limp hand on Nur's chest.

Across the barriers of pain that sundered him from everyone, Nur strained to touch his friend, but his regret for his failures held him back.

He sighed and closed his eyes for a moment.

In a flash he could see the cool mango-groves where he had gone with Gama. The boy had been kind to him, getting him baskets of fruits from the gardeners to bring home, but he used to beat other people viciously. From the time Gama had left school, why even before that, because he was the son of a vegetable stall-keeper in Chowk Farid, one of the most disreputable quarters of the town, the violence of his deeds had become legendary, and Nur had never really regarded his friend's life as in any way consistent with inner goodness, and had always been afraid of his hooliganism. The hulking shape of the boy's huge frame and the profession he had adopted after years of vagabondage were against him too, and Nur recalled how often, since going to college, he had cut him so as not to get a bad name. Now he felt his own superiority lie like a blot upon his heart...

'Nur, little one, may I go and fetch the Doctor?' Gama asked with a broken voice.

'No, you sit here and talk to me a little — that is, if you are not losing fares all the time,' Nur said. 'The Doctor will soon come on his morning visit, and then you can go.'

'Are you sure you don't feel bad?' Gama asked.

'Yes, I am all right,' Nur said, seeking to ease the strain he felt in accepting the gesture of his friend's tenderness. 'You know,' he continued, to excuse his separateness, 'the physical exhaustion leaves me so apathetic that I feel as if my back was broken.'

But even as he said so he knew that it was the hardening of his heart through his disillusionment and not the apathy that made him incapable of lifting his hand from under the sheet and putting it into Gama's.

'It is strange that you say:

> 'Why did you drag me into the dust by making me an M.A.?'

Gama said to overcome the sudden gulf between them. 'Didn't you like going to college? I...' But he didn't finish what he was going to say: that though he had made capital out of his failures at school and his consequent inability to go to college by developing a roughness of action and passion, he would have liked to have gone through a long educational course if only to evade the responsibility of having to earn a living for some more years, especially as one could indulge in any vice and never get a bad name if only one disguised oneself under the name of 'student.'

'Yes, brother,' Nur said and then, sensing the reason for Gama's hesitation, added, 'The unattainable seems great. But if you are poor you can't get anywhere; if you can't keep pace with the fashions invented by the rich students, they dub you mean and cut you. *Achha,* there couldn't be any worse snobbery in the world than that of the...' And he impatiently twisted his face as if the very thought of poverty evoked in him a kind of disgust, and there was the knowledge of all the little pinpricks and humiliations to his self-respect that he had suffered because he was a confectioner's son.

For a moment he lay confused. Then he felt his temples throb with the fretting and he tried to calm himself by looking away. His eyes stared at the dilapidated ceiling where the cobwebs hung to their nets among the thick coils of soot, and his face seemed to become enchantingly childlike, as if it had never suffered the pang of a sigh.

'It was a lucky escape from the prison of that school, where I had always been afraid of being beaten,' he said smiling. 'Nobody could beat you at college and the professors treated everyone as gentlemen. And in a way it was as Azad might have said,

> 'a golden summer during which I plucked the blossoms
> from the orchards of many colourful nights and days...'

'Oh, you mean Azad, the Teddy Sahib, who was your friend, the son of the Health Officer who went mad because he failed to become a deputy collector. Or do you mean the poet, Maulana Muhammad

Husein Azad?' Gama asked with a slight trace of mockery in his voice.

'I mean Teddy,' Nur said wistfully. 'Isn't it terrible that he should go off his head? He was a marvel, you know...'

'He must have been, that's why he went mad, I suppose,' said Gama with a trace of malice. He had been jealous of Nur's friendship with Azad.

'No, really, Gamian,' Nur said, rising excitedly to the defence of his friend, 'he was the only friend I made at college, and he was really wonderful. He was driven to madness by people and our kind of bullock's life...' He opened his mouth to say something loudly, but thought better of it and sank back, coughing, biting his lips and churning the froth in his mouth.

Gama rubbed his chest slowly, soothingly and contemplated his face, rather frightened. But Nur opened his eyes, breathed a few deep breaths and smiling, lay still for a moment and said: 'Since the last few days, I have been getting these choking breaths. Yesterday my breathing was better, but I don't know why I am gasping this morning.'

'You must not worry about anyone,' Gama said, 'You must lie still.'

'I am all right,' Nur said slowly. 'And really I must tell you about poor Azad. You never liked him, you see, you didn't meet him. He was really maddened by our kind of existence... I remember that the first time I saw him come up to college, dressed in his khaki shirt, shorts, and khaki polo topee, an impetuous little fellow, on a rusty old bicycle, I thought the same as you... But the older boys were making fun of the first year fools and they hid Azad's bicycle and his hat when he went to see the Principal. And when he came out they ragged him by making rude noises, as he looked for his belongings. He could see it in their eyes that they had hidden the things and he asked them smilingly to give them to him. But they refused to own up and just mocked. You would have been sorry for him if you had been there and you would have admired what he did. He challenged them all and fell upon them. I have never seen anything like it — the glint of fire in his eyes when the boys became indecent... He leapt upon them with a quivering face... I knew that none of them would dare to attack me because of you, and I rescued him and showed him where his hat and bicycle were. It was because of that that we became friends and not as people maliciously said later that we had formed a "conspiracy of beloveds." He was a very affectionate person...'

Gama bent his head with the silent shame of a memory of a year ago when he himself had mocked at Azad, crying out in the bazaar, '*Hai* Babu*ji*,' with a rude simulation of the tone of a lover sighing for his beloved.

'He was fond of making speeches,' Nur said, remembering an evening when Azad had lifted him out of his loneliness by his speech when he won the Ruchi Ram Sahni Declamation Prize, remembering the very colour, and the ring of those words of Azad's, when with a face transfigured with eagerness he had summed up the universe.

' "The whole world is in search of happiness," he used to say,' Nur began.

'What then?' Gama asked.

Nur paused embarrassedly on the edge of the words as they rang in his ears across the space of six years. He didn't want to repeat them, as they might easily lend themselves to Gama's mockery, and yet he couldn't restrain himself.

'The whole world is in search of happiness,' he repeated, loudly, though he knew for certain from the light in Gama's eyes that if he would not mock, he would certainly not be able to understand the whole meaning of those words. 'The whole world is in search of happiness, all mankind seeks the privileges of glory and power and wealth. But it is vulgar, I tell you, it is vulgar and stupid, the way in which society distributes her favours. The bitch has no morals. She yields herself to the embraces of any robber, brigand or cheating idiot who has secured for himself the traditional right to a vested interest. And these conscienceless swines have forgotten death, the cancer which grows slowly and surely within them, the cancer of their own decay, the germ of their own decay that they bear within them; and they shall be annihilated long before they have earned their pensions or retired to enjoy their ill-gotten gains...'

Nur paused to look at Gama and to see if he were listening to the words. Gama's attention was drifting but Nur went on nevertheless as if he were talking aloud to himself.

' "But death comes to everyone, you will say, gentlemen," he had himself posed the question and then burst out with that querulous impatience which characterised him: "Yes, yes, death comes to everyone, but there are two ways of avoiding it. Some form silent conspiracy to forget it; they are the imbeciles who build on graft and extortion and cunning and sheer might and so blacken their souls in the struggle for self-aggrandisement that they daren't enjoy the gains of their perfidy, and who therefore combine holiness with business like our *Lallas,* and talk of the things of the spirit even as they pass the hand of satisfaction over their bellies. And then, there are the men who are willing to accept a share in the total gain of the struggle for existence of the community, who want to organise the fight against nature, and who, though afraid of death, seek to conquer it... They will..." I don't remember the rest,' Nur said faltering and flushed but exhilarated as if his soul was dancing to the sound of that rhetoric with a recklessness which frightened him.

'You have said the truth, "Why did you drag me in the dust by making me an M.A." ' said Gama quoting the beginning of Nur's poem against Azad.

'But really, really, believe me,' said Nur, 'I know he went mad because the torn and battered soul of India was struggling inside him, because he seemed to have understood the hopelessness of our lot. Really, he knew and suffered. We used to talk during our long walks, and it is curious that we felt we knew what was wrong with India and with ourselves, but couldn't do anything, and only sank deeper and deeper into despair. I must say I owe him a great deal...'

'Your illness, for instance,' said Gama.

'No, really,' protested Nur. 'It may be that he awakened me to the misery of our condition and made me suffer, but he also released all the stifled impulses I had never suspected in myself before...' And he was going to say that Azad had made him talk as he had never talked before, laugh, weep, read, think, feel, do things, live and breathe to a new rhythm, that he had broken all the barriers of self-consciousness that separated him, the confectioner's son, from everyone else, but he felt he was being naive and Gama was antagonistic. And yet he couldn't restrain himself from resuscitating the truth about Azad in an attempt to obliterate Gama's prejudice: 'He initiated me into the mysteries of poetry and philosophy,' he continued, sweating in the warm glare of the sun that burnt hotly outside now. 'It was really the way he talked. The passion, for instance, which he put into the reading of books, suiting his intonation to the slow gradation of Heine's love poems, to the lyrics of Goethe and Iqbal, to the broad histrionic gesture of Mercutio in *Romeo and Juliet,* to the comic overtones of Dickens and the polished undertones of Flaubert, all names to you, as they were to me, because the only literature I had known was the *High-roads of History* and Southey's *Life of Nelson* which I had read for the Matric,

Rawlinson's *Selection of Essays* and selections from Boswell's *Life of Johnson* which were the texts for the first and second year at college, and the cribs and questions and answers by Sheikh Abdul Qadir... I don't know where he got to know all these things...'

'Perhaps he didn't know them at all and it was really the way he talked,' said Gama laughing.

'No,' Nur said, 'he spent most of his time in odd corners of the college, while all of us just wasted our time ragging each other and gossiping as we sat in the fields outside the college buildings during the free hours. You see, the boys who passed out from our school, specially Sarjit and Mathra, formed a group and they resented my friendship with Azad. But when I went and sat with Sarjit and company they only talked scandal about which boy was in love with whom, and what Professor had an alliance with which boy, and whether so and so shouldn't be ragged if he came that way, and what time they would get to the club, for tennis and ping-pong. One day I decided to break away from that crowd and joined Azad who was sitting writing poetry in the dome of the college. And he opened my eyes to realities.'

'Childling, you are easily led astray,' said Gama, out of a clash of kindness for Nur, a contempt for Azad and a sense of inferiority. 'All those speeches of his are no use. We want a worker's raj just as it is prevailing in Russia, because the condition here will be as it is in Russia. There was a time when the Czar ruled Russia as the Badshah of Vilayat rules us. But one day he was shot down. And the peasants and labourers are ruling there. I have joined a tonga-wallahs' branch of the Labour Federation. The labourers of Hindustan are realising that the Sarkar can't go on.

'*Ohe bachu,* you will be put into prison,' Nur said, laughing but earnest.

'I don't care for the limp lord,' said Gama with a swagger. But then he smiled embarrassedly as if he were not sure of himself.

Nur looked at a feather dropping from the top of a house across the shadow which cut the fierce sun outside, and he saw the shimmering of an azure and scarlet and yellow spectrum of light before him as he had often done lying in this bed. He felt the monotony of his existence and the ceaseless discomfort which his body had endured through the burning sun. The only high spots had been those baths in the canal with Azad when they were at college, or the times when they had lifted their heads towards the clotted greenery of the city gardens, specially when they had worked together for their finals. Otherwise, one commonplace day had followed another, the oppressive daylight sucking the strength out of one's bones and leaving one weak and tired and uninterested. It was perhaps the heat which made him so apathetic now... 'But it is no use thinking of that,' he said to himself, 'it only makes me impatient.' And he turned to Gama, though he knew that the lengthy conversation was straining him.

'Have you heard how Azad is now?' he asked. 'And is he still in the asylum or has he been brought back to his father's house?'

'They say he was brought back from the asylum,' answered Gama, 'but he became violent again, raved profanities and obscenities and went on a hunger strike like Gandhi, demanding the release not only of all political prisoners but of all lunatics...'

'You are joking,' Nur said, 'I suppose the Government brought influence to bear on his father... If only he hadn't been such a fool, airing his opinions when even the boldest spirits spoke in guarded undertones, but he was always so impetuous...' And he thought of the fiery, fanatical figure, at times like a sword that was never sheathed and destroyed everything in its way, and at others, loose and reckless, with a hearty laugh that made the world seem like a coloured bubble through its drumming thunders, and plunged one into a welter of confusion. Such a person, maddened by the life that surrounded him. Why didn't he go on writing poetry? Why did he have to go into politics? But what self-respecting person in India could help being political; who could help being affected by the sordid side of this tragic existence? He himself had kept his mouth shut but what had he got? Why, he had known as he left college that death lurked for him at the bend of the road...

'What are you thinking?' Gama asked, turning uncomfortably to prepare for his departure.

'Only these memories of our past,' Nur said wearily.

'But why do you feel like that this morning?' Gama said. 'You are as peevish as a stubborn child. Come, have a heart. You will be all right.'

'My father wanted me to apply for admission to all the Government services,' said Nur in an even, cynical voice, 'to all the Government services, one after another, believing that since I had got a degree I had a free ticket for admission into the paradise of officialdom. And, in anticipation of my future position as a dignified member of the Government of India, he married me off. You should have seen the bustle and uproar in this house, the raucous laughter of the women of the gulley as they sang filthy songs on the top of the house ...And the crowds of guests gorging on the sweets, which the Chaudhri made, as they had never gorged before... You should have seen their paunches expand with the free food — and the paunch of Maulvi Shahab Din knew no bounds. The noise and the din amid the sweating bodies left no room for one to stand or sit and it was sheer bedlam till the day when they led two sheep to be martyred before the divines and the witnesses... And I nearly died of shame to think what my college friends would feel. But of course, I had to go through the absurd ritual for fear that the Chaudhri would lose his temper in public...

That poor, silly girl, Iqbal, was as much a pawn in the game which her father was playing with mine as I was in the game which my father was playing with her's; her father thought that I would get into the Imperial Service with my first class degree, and my father thought that the daughter of a respectable veterinary surgeon would bring a good dowry. And both the players were deceived in deceiving each other. I could not get into the Imperial Service and she only brought the prestige of her father's position, and her own self, for the dowry. But no one realised this until after I returned from the interview with the board which was to select candidates for the Imperial Forest Service.

I never told you of this but, through the confusion of hope and fear I spent myself like a fool, arranging the details of a plan to hide my origin because that was the only obstacle to my selection since I had passed well from the University. It was very funny... I could laugh at it now... I borrowed a suit from Azad and a brown, trilby hat, as the Chaudhri wouldn't believe that it was necessary to buy me a Sahib's rigout such as could compete with the Ranken and Company suits of the other candidates; the Chaudhri didn't see why a suit was necessary at all since I was an M.A. Pass... But, of course, he didn't know that jobs are given by the Public Service Commission for smartness, general appearance, the possession of a good pedigree and according to the number of testimonials and recommendations from influential persons that a man may have, more than for anything else. You should have seen me doing a dress rehearsal before going to Simla...'

'You must have looked like a Sahib, with your fair complexion,' commented Gama with admiration.

'Yes, I must confess,' said Nur flushing with fatigue and excitement, though his voice was still tuned to a smooth cynicism, 'for once I liked myself, whereas otherwise I had always been embarrassed by the number of lovers who made my life difficult at school and college. But the shame of knowing that I was the son of a confectioner, if I am to be honest, lessened the thrill of my own perfection. I never looked at my face in the glass afterwards without casting my eyes on my feet also immediately, like the peacock who weeps to see its ugly paws, and so I went... The journey to Simla — oh, I shall never forget that journey to Simla — I suppose it was the best thing I got out of it all. And the hotel, though since I knew that the Chaudhri had borrowed the hundred rupees for my expenses I couldn't enjoy the *Angrezi* food they gave us at the Hotel Bristol. And then the interview. . . The fear almost gave me dysentery.'

He paused, laughed nervously and reddened, then paled with shame.

'Go on,' Gama said impatiently. 'Tell me about that. Did you see the *Lat* Sahib?'

'Long before I saw the *Lat* Sahib, there were those sons of the *Lats* who were appearing before the board. You can't imagine the feeling I had when I entered the waiting room at Barnes Court, the office of the Governor of the Punjab: there were thirty other candidates, all splendidly dressed in expensive suits, all obviously the sons of the richest of fathers. And I had to make a terrible effort in my own mind not to betray my feelings during that long ordeal...'

He stopped short suddenly as if he felt suffocated with the lack of air in the low-ceilinged room and he moved his legs about as if he wanted to jump out of bed, and escape into the open...

'Then what happened?' asked Gama who had never been inside an Englishman's house or talked to a European, except that he had been caned by Mercado, the Head Master of the Islamia School.

'Oh, nothing very much,' said Nur, his face twisting with a wry smile as if he were writhing with impatience inside and yet making a desperate effort to spit it out now that he had begun to vomit out his suffering. 'The dramatic entry of me, in a complete funk, into the room where the commission sat, under the guidance of a peon in a goldbraided redcoat, who not only looked like a Rajah but behaved insolently like one; the seriousness of that moment, in which tables, curtains, papers, pens and an assortment of the *Lat* Sahib's pipes swam in the void before my eyes with the glorious polished air of perfection surrounding them and, of course, as if it just had to happen at that auspicious moment, the foolish blunder on my part in kicking a chair over and saying "Good Noon," when I should have said, " Good Morning"...'

He blushed with embarrassment at telling Gama the story of his folly and exposing himself in the most sensitive, vulnerable parts of his character, and he lingered on the tremulous chords of that tense moment when his greeting was returned and when fear had taken possession of his body and set it trembling.

'You know, that man Bailey was the son of a swine,' he continued, after a little hesitation. 'He was so alert in observation, one of those Englishmen who know us better than we know ourselves. My life went out of me as I saw his lean, wily face, lined on the cheeks as if he had been sucked up like an orange by that cow of a wife of his. I couldn't understand the first question he asked me because the soft tone of his measured speech seemed to me to be issuing from the steady stare of his eyes rather than from his mouth. I don't think his colleagues understood the burr-burr of his thin lips either, as they sat round him like statues; the buffalo-faced Raja Ram Singh, the parrot-nosed Abdul Hamid Khan, and that lover of his mother, the Parsi, Sir Fredoonji. I could have laughed had I not been terror-stricken by the *Lat* Sahib, the long-necked pelican. I have never known the eternities of hell in this life as in those moments...'

He stopped again and drowsed through a suffering in which the present was interweaving with the past. And, for a moment, he listened to his heart drumming like a tom-tom in a monotonous rhythm.

'We ought to beat them with our shoes soaked in water, these illegally begotten, the limp lords as well as their sycophants!' said Gama, whose hooliganism had become the desperate sincerity of political passion roused by the struggle in the dust, the straw, the dung, the urine of the underworld in which he lived.

'Oh, what is the use?' Nur said as he turned his face away, tired and worn and grey, as if he were a creature from another world, a pale traveller from some distant country, who had a story to tell which he thought wouldn't be understood by any man of this land, and who was yet impelled by a curious instinct to unburden himself as if he would talk himself out of his frustration.

'Abdul Hamid Khan is a fanatical Muslim Leaguer, isn't he?' Gama asked.

'But I had known from the very beginning that I wouldn't be accepted,' Nur said in a hopeless, low voice, and stopped for a moment to consider how to convey his humiliation so as not to be unkind to himself and to expose his judges the more cruelly in order to revenge himself upon them. 'When Raja Ram Singh asked me whether I had taken part in any "extramural" activity at college, I was so surprised at the buffalo-face mouthing a difficult word that I knew he had looked at the dictionary before coming there. And, frankly, I didn't know the meaning of the word myself, though I tried to make a vague guess and answered I had played tennis. And Abdul Hamid Khan's sympathy for his Mohammedan co-religionists refused to appear. Instead, the pig-eater laughed when Fredoonji asked me if my father was a confectioner, and I said: "Oh, no sir, he is the Chaudhri of the bazaar..." And so I walked away from the house of the limp lord! And as the poet has said: "I came out of your lane very insulted and humiliated." '

He had a stale taste at the root of his palate as he ended on that note and clicked his tongue against the roof of his mouth to take away the dryness that the profusion of speech had produced. And he became conscious of the incommunicability of his feelings to Gama or to anybody, through the impatience that possessed him.

But even as he relaxed, his bitterness returned. Only this time instead of bursting out, he simulated the air of stretching his limbs and twisted about on the bed as if to exercise the fatigue that possessed him.

'You are very restless,' said Gama. 'Are your limbs tired? May I press your legs?'

'No, I feel slightly cold,' Nur said.

'I must be going now,' Gama suddenly said, listening to the air. 'Someone is coming up the stairs.'

'Nur, Nur, my son,' a heavy hoarse voice came with the puffing and panting of hosts of other women, and after a long moment, the short, square form of his mother-in-law emerged, shrouded in her flowing white cotton veil, followed by the shrouded ghosts of his wife and her aunt.

'Hai, hai,' they cried as they advanced, 'here is a man.' And dropping the thick shrouds they had lifted to get a view of Nur, they rushed like fluttering, frightened hens towards a corner of the room.

Thereupon Gama turned and without looking this side or that, rushed away, down the stairs, lest the modesty of the women be outraged by the penetration of his glance.

'Ohe Gamian!' Nur shouted, jumping from his bed till his skeleton bent over his ribs, *'Ohe...'* And then, realising that his

friend was out of hearing he coughed with the strain of the effort as if every sinew and fibre of his skin were snapping with the black cough which tugged at his tissues, and tore the very protoplasm of his life. He hung his head down and bit his lips and resigned himself to the tides of the cough that lashed his inside, till the convulsive spasms subsided into gasps of hiccupping breaths and, bringing tears to his eyes, reddening his face a vivid red, threw up thick globules of blood and saliva like a string of tattered rags.

'Oh! my mother, oh! my mother,' he moaned through the acrid droolings, of his pain, and bending over the spittoon to throw off the last streaks of saliva in his mouth strained his neck to breathe. . .

'Hai, hai! Hai, hai!' the two elderly women shrieked rushing towards him like vultures to their prey and wailed: 'What will happen to us, what will happen to our Iqbal?' while his girl wife stood at the foot of the bed, unhooded and helpless, with tears in her eyes.

Nur lay back with his eyes closed.

'Hai, hai!, Hai, hai!' his mother-in-law and her sister cried the more loudly, and beating their breasts, howled and moaned till the old Grandma came slowly down the stairs and the women of the neighbouring houses rushed to the windows of their houses and began to shout, 'Is he dead? Is he dead?'

Nur was oppressed by the hysterical women, embarrassed and exasperated by the way they had lighted upon him when he was talking to Gama and broken the spell of his indignation against the world, which was forcing out of him the truths that he had felt but never expressed, which was making him recognise the necessity to tell life what he thought of it, now that he was to be deprived of it...

The women's wails grew louder and shriller as his grandmother, his stepmother and the other women of the lane joined the chorus, the loudest of them adding to their shrieks a violent show of beating their breasts and smiting their foreheads in a rhythmic sequence attuned to the dirge of *Hai, hai! Hai, hai! Hai, hai!*

Nur hardened his jaws, stiffened his body, rose as if he were a brittle sword which wanted to hack their sprawling forms. But even as he lifted his head, he realised the futility of his rage against them as they were only practising a stupid convention that ordained the invocation of cries and shrieks and howls at the barest sign of death. He merely opened his eyes and waved his arm and said: 'I am not dead, I am not dead,' and collapsed in a heap.

'Be quiet, mother! Be quiet, auntie! Be quiet, grandma!' his wife was saying, as she struggled to stop them beating their breasts.

Nur looked at her. She seemed so helpless and shy that he felt sick to think he had ever hated her, she seemed so touching in her stupidity that he wished he could touch her now and make a contact which he had refused to establish between himself and her ever since they had been married, except in the moments of lust when she had docilely opened her legs to him.

'Come mother, come auntie, come grandma, let him rest, come,' she was whispering, as she dragged them away one by one. And she seemed to him tenderer than ever, someone who had hidden the light of her affection and her love in her own distress always, someone who had suffered and yet never shown it by word or deed. He suddenly recalled that he had cruelly and deliberately detached himself from her, because she was restrained by the convention of purdah, because she wasn't a fashionable woman who could put on a sari and walk out with him so that he could proudly show her off to the world as his wife, and he was full of remorse. For, during the days of his suffering, the dull, hot days which followed his degradation at the hands of the selection committee of the

Imperial Forest Service, when he had walked the dusty roads from one Government office to another, in midsummer heat, and was insulted by the peons who refused to let him see officials because he couldn't pay them gratuities, she had followed him about tenderly, pathetically, fetching him cool drinks and fanning him, pressing his head, rubbing his feet, soothing him as he sought to forget the weariness of his struggle for a job in an afternoon's sleep. And he had kicked her in the chagrin of his disappointments when, one day, during the period when he wrote a hundred applications and trudged a thousand weary miles to secure recommendations, during the days when he was weeping over the sneers of his relatives and the whispered mockery of the neighbours, she had yielded to him the perplexing knowledge of her pregnancy. And even then she had followed him about, like a devoted dog, worshipping him with her eyes, while he, in the panic of the fear of fatherhood that hung like an extra load on his already heavy-laden head, had frowned at her, refused to talk to her, and ignored her utterly, only charging at her now and then with the deliberate, violent, hard thrusts of a diabolical passion, as if he wanted to revenge himself against her... and leave her high and dry in the writhings of dissatisfaction without a word or a gesture of consolation... And when she had proudly presented him with the gift of a little red-faced girl child who frowned and cried with closed eyes, he had felt like murdering her and the child and had gone out reading among the tall valerians of the city garden, its towers and its lawns.

'What is it, my son?' his grandmother pouted in a short-breathed drawl, as she came trembling and shaking back to him with the eternal tears in her eyes. 'What is it then? May I be your sacrifice!'

Disturbed in the flow of his thoughts he looked at her in a dazed, absent-minded stare. Then he looked straight across her to where his wife stood after sending the other women upstairs and smiled a weak, helpless smile at her, wishing she would come and put her arms round him. But the slight, pale, irregular face of the girl was impassive, as if she were still frightened of him.

'Iqbal,' he said to summon her to him.

The girl lifted her innocent, downcast, brown eyes, but just that moment the old woman began to stroke his head and murmur: 'Go to sleep, my child, may I be your sacrifice! Those fainthearted women frightened me.'

And moving aside with bent back she said, 'Come, Iqbal, you come and rest too, my daughter. Come, my child, why didn't you bring the baby?'

'She is coming with my other aunt, grandma,' Iqbal said, and then she looked towards her husband, as if imploring him with her eyes to call her again.

Nur's eyes were averted, however. Someone had suddenly come in between them, some ugly, horrible fate which had intervened to isolate them, as it had always done, till their eyes had never met in the nakedness of a common light, and now there was no building up of a private relationship between them, for now he was far removed from everyone.

If it had not been for the weight of responsibilities that had been piling up, he thought to himself as he saw her turn her back and follow grandma, if life had not buried him under the weight of his duties as a son, a husband and as a father, he might have loved her... But poverty... Oh! how it had hardened him to life, how it had made him insensitive to the colours, the shapes, the forms of things, to the thoughts, the feelings of people, till he had no contact with anyone or anything and went irritably through the world without any perception of even the lumps of human existence, to say nothing of the subtle nuances of experience... poverty had come between him and her, how cruel it had made him to her, how stubbornly aloof and hard, so that now when he wanted to smile at her, to touch her, he had turned his eyes away, frozen and rigid, too proud and too ashamed to look at her, to yield... And it was all his father's doing...

'The son of Sheikh Pir Baksh has become a deputy collector, why can't you? The son of Sardar Kalyan Singh has become a sub-judge, why can't you?' Those words and the searching gleam of the Chaudhri's blood-streaked eyes had spread a terror in his soul till he had felt that every breath he breathed was in jeopardy, that every morsel of food he ate in the house was being watched.

And, afraid of the penalties he might have to pay for disobedience, he had put his heart and soul into the work necessary for the I.C.S... But only he knew what he had gone through, waking up with aching eyelids in the dawn and getting down to work by the light of that kerosene lamp after washing his face in the water of *amlas*... sighing over every second page as he felt hopeless about his success in the competition. Those long summer months of work... He had felt like being in a prison of books... The date of the examination hanging like the sword of Damocles over his head... The misery of ten hours a day while all the world laughed, played and went about as usual... He used to cover his head with wet towels to keep himself from going mad with the heat... But he had known that this city would follow him, the streets of this city which had grown stale and horrible from the familiarity of being seen in the glare of the sun, day after day, for years, the streets of the city in which everyone knew him and whispered as he passed by, 'there goes Nur, the son of the confectioner who is an M.A. Pass, but who sits idle, with one hand on the other, and kills flies because he can't get a job.' And he knew that the flower-seller lane in Dhab-Khatikan of this city would direct his footsteps within its narrow purlieus by the children who sat excreting in the drain and the women who sat spinning or weaving garlands in lightless hovels; he would grow grey and die in his father's hateful house; fate had shattered his will to live, he really wanted to die and would never be able to escape; the foul breath he breathed here had poisoned him, so that he would take the bitter taste of its air about with him wherever he went till the poison would work its way slowly into his entire system and destroy him...

And, true to his prognostications, being a confectioner's son, he had only secured five marks in the viva and failed to get into the I.C.S. in spite of the other high marks... And for months he had gone about living in a dead and lightless world with the winds of his father's temper raging against the dark walls of his mind... And he had wished for release, longed for it, prayed for it, for each day he had awakened to recognise himself still breathing... till he had just ceased to care, gone beyond suffering to a listlessness and apathy like that of the first days of his illness, and as if there was no meaning in anything, that one just drifted along anyhow, hoping for little, believing less, and committed to one's breath because one hadn't the courage to take one's life and end it all.

Then, as the last remaining desire in life, he had wished between periods of hopelessness and blank despair and endless, bottomless misery for the gift of a little job, howsoever insignificant and humiliating, even the job of a peon if it were not in this city, so that he could earn a little bread for himself, Iqbal and the child.... But even this last little wish was not to be fulfilled easily... Only days and unending days morning, noon and night and the rub of his father's abuse and curses with every morsel of bread and every bite at a bone... And months... Oh where could one hide one's face?... Where could one go?... For when it came to the point one couldn't even go and become a boot-black in a different town as the news would spread, and there was still a lingering pride left in one's body, pride and the fear of being laughed at by the world, of being beaten and insulted by the Chaudhri... One only had to eat a little food and this stupid pride came creeping back into one, the pride of one's manhood and the pride of being an educated, intelligent man, a Babu, an MA Pass... The world was so snobbish, and one was so afraid of doing the wrong thing all the time. '...*Ohe,* look at that Nur, the son of the confectioner; he fancied himself as a Babu, and now he has come down to his real state, become a coolie.' Any kind of manual labour was bad, was low and unworthy. It wasn't respectable to exert one's hands... the only *izzat* was in Government service... And it wasn't only that the outside world believed this, the trouble was, if one was honest, that one had begun to believe in the snobbery oneself and was ashamed and embarrassed...

Then, at last, after the exertions of his father-in-law, after the abject crawling of his father with joined hands before that Bhai Bhachanga Singh, Inspector of Post Offices, after all the influence, brought to bear on Sheikh Pir Baksh, the Minister of Education, after all the recommendations, a clerkship in the Post Office at twenty rupees, and lucky to get it, as fifteen MA's and a hundred and thirty-seven BA's had applied for the same post, and but for the wire pulling, the favouritism for the Mohammedan and all the other influences, he would never have got it...

And then he lay still, listening to his own breath as if he were fascinated by his own naivete, saying to himself, 'Strange, it's my pain... the pain I can't understand... of which I am going to die. Doesn't hurt really... I feel no different from what I have felt for months... a little better, a little worse... I must be dying...'

The disappointment had done it, the routine of that office, working with dingy clerks, when the hours weighed like lead... selling postage stamps when he might have been an Imperial Service Officer...

Was he ungrateful to feel doomed though?

He looked into his heart with the inner eye and asked whether there was nothing in all the flux of his life that could have relieved his doom, no beauty, no tenderness, no faith, nothing but foiled desire...

There was no answer.

Only a slight tremor turned into perspiration, and the weakness of his body was sucked by the heat, and the heavy eyelids closed in stupor, against his will, conjuring queer images: Tarzan was lifting the woman, her golden hair streaming... Myrna Loy, perfect featured, and William Powell with a face like any He-man's... Wonderful white houses in the English style... Charlie Chaplin running after the new woman he had seen on the corner of the restless street, all for love, a new love...

He felt his heart throbbing with a helpless pity for himself, that he had never fallen in love, that he had not gone to England as a probationer of the Imperial Forest Service or the LCS and come back to live a life in the English style, but lay completing the circuit of his life, fading into the unknown, into a future where there seemed to be a dearth even of past memories, where even the facts of his present state were slipping...

'What had happened and what was happening?... Nothing... the Doctor will be coming soon...'

'It was my perverse pride that denied Iqbal's feelings,' he said to himself, 'and sent her away to her father's house... Even the playful smile on the face of Rashida whom my sperm had made, did not move me...'

In his recoil, he frowned and wriggled and then, turning in upon himself, said, 'Oh, it couldn't be helped...'

He listened intently to the silence, controlling his breath for a moment... The blood was pumping into the veins and the arteries seemed swollen and hard... Perhaps they were affected by the heat...

But there was no doubt... Life was ebbing in him. It was a matter of days...

That first haemorrhage had been a surprise to him... He had taken the shock calmly... But now it was no easy matter to sleep over it, for it might be a question of hours... He felt afraid.

But he mustn't get excited, else the Doctor would complain. He must be calm, above all things, calm. Look how calm he had been for days... Why, the Doctor had complemented him on his ability to notice each symptom of the disease.

He recalled the changing phases of his body, while he felt his pulse... One day... it was a month ago, he had felt bad, very bad... But then he had felt well, and had even read Charles Garvice. It was curious how, when he was reading books, the festoons of clothes, the hurricane lamp hanging by the wall, and all the jumble of things which looked ugly in the ordinary light assumed a certain grandeur. The next day he had not been so well, and he felt apathetic to everyone and everything. His breathing had been heavy as it was now, and his fever was rising, and he had moaned exactly as he had done today. Perhaps he was trying grimly to hold on to himself, but what was the use, the cure was outside himself, and why couldn't he get out of the prison of his own broodings... But there was nothing else to do...

It was no use looking to anything outside of himself for help... For he felt so exhausted, lying there. Why couldn't he wrestle with every moment and delay the end for a few months, for a few years...? By prayer, for instance. That had given him whole days of good health... What a boon it was; he had liked people. 'I wonder if the attacks of haemorrhage come because I don't pray any more...' But that was stupid! What was he thinking about? Neither God nor the Devil could help him...

A gleam of kindliness coloured his face for a moment, then changed to a frown, and he turned his tired body again, and shrank back like a snail into his own skin.

That haemorrhage, a fortnight ago, was the worst he had had. His disease had surely begun to overpower him then. He had been terrified... But, after all, it could not have done him much harm. It couldn't have done, because he had felt life in his body... Why, the blood had rushed to his cheeks and that ghastly pallor of months had gone... But for the chill that he caught at dawn last Thursday... How he had trembled: always he had trembled when he had had fever, even as a child, a soft tremor went shivering through the nerves of his body. The cold had affected him badly, because he had had a terrible haemorrhage on Saturday... How helpless he had felt till the Doctor prescribed arsenic... But on Sunday his depression had lifted. He could rise again from the ashes... Yesterday he had felt that too, and today... He was tired perhaps, but he would get up, in spite of the haemorrhage, this morning. Would he though? Could he?... after months of sinking life? Could he? Hark, there was someone...

He listened.

There was the Doctor. They were Captain Pochanwala's footsteps. He must ask him. He must get ready, not shuffle the clothes, lie still...

'Well, Mr. Nur, how are you this morning?' asked Captain Pochanwala superciliously, advancing into the room with an urbane manner which he seemed to have cultivated specially to suit the distinctive fawn-coloured polo topee which he alone of all the Indians in Amritsar wore with his well-cut suit. Being a Parsi, he perhaps thought himself superior to all the other Indians who had begun to wear English clothes.

Nur strained to say, 'Good morning,' but his father appeared behind the Doctor, and, somehow, he felt ashamed to be speaking English in the presence of the Chaudhri, as it would seem like showing off.

'Flushed, very flushed, breathing bad,' the Doctor said and fixing his gaze on Nur he asked, 'How is the cough?'

'Better,' said Nur, and he saw his father going upstairs, presumably to fetch the money for the Doctor's fees, since Captain Pochanwala didn't believe in credit and had asked for his remuneration even when he had arrived too late to cure Nur's mother.

'Let us see the temperature!' the Doctor said, screwing up his eyes and nose as if he really didn't want to come into contact with his patient.

And while Nur was drawing his hand out of the sheet, Captain Pochanwala looked contemptuously round the room, and then put his hand on the boy's forehead.

'Very hot, very hot, very hot!' he said, 'What have you been doing to excite yourself this morning?'

'Nothing, Doctor,' said Nur.

Captain Pochanwala was applying the stethoscope to his patient's heart, and didn't wait for the boy to answer.

'Hum...' he said rather abstractedly and twisting his lower lips coldly and looking at the boy with knitted brows and eyes turned sideways, 'that intractable lung... any haemorrhage this morning?'

'No,' said Nur, then correcting himself, 'Yes.'

Captain Pochanwala looked quizzically about him and contemplated the purple glow on the boy's face for a moment...

'There is some medicine there, isn't there?' he asked and then turning to the table himself confirmed, 'Yes.'

'How is he, Doctor Sahib?' asked the Chaudhri coming down the stairs, grim and heavy.

'I am afraid Mr. Nur has been exciting himself,' Captain Pochanwala replied, putting away his stethoscope. 'He should remain absolutely quiet. That medicine in the bottle will do for some days...' Then he took out his watch and moved towards the door, beckoning the Chaudhri.

Nur didn't know whether the Doctor had made his gesture to tell his father confidentially that it was the end or whether to make sure of his fee... From the way in which he extended his hand, it seemed he was just a little embarrassed at the heartlessness of his demand for his fee; but then, as he took the five rupee note, he whispered something to the Chaudhri.

'Will you come in again this evening, Sarkar?' asked the Chaudhri as the Doctor was adjusting his hat so as not to knock it against the narrow door of the stairs.

But Captain Pochanwala affected not to have heard and screwing up his nose, opening his eyes wide, had explored the comparative darkness.

'What did the *Dagdar* say?' Nur heard his grandmother ask from where she came scrambling down the stairs again.

'Nothing very much,' the Chaudhri replied casually unheeding. Then he turned to Nur and asked sneeringly: 'What have you been doing to yourself, *ohe, Gentermana*?'

'How much more alive his patients are to the case histories of their ailments,' said Nur, as if he were talking aloud to himself, 'than Captain Pochanwala. He thrives on the snobbery of his position as an ex-IMS Officer. But he only had a temporary commission during the war, and doesn't know any other medicines except quinine and tincture of iodine.'

'What have you done,' the Chaudhri burst out, red with rage, 'that you should be critical of your elders? You wasted hundreds of rupees of my hard-earned money, you son of a bitch, and you couldn't even get a job to feed yourself and wife and child? Why don't you die of shame, you lover of your mother, and rid me of the responsibility you have imposed on me so long? When will you die, you dog? How long will you go on prolonging the agony of your poor old grandmother? You have disgraced me and given a bad name to your family! Go to hell and die and be done with it, you wretch...'

'My son, my son, what are you saying?' the old woman appealed coming towards the Chaudhri with lifted, supplicating hands.

'Go to hell and be done with it, die and rid us all of this responsibility...' the Chaudhri shouted raising his voice, 'Die and give me peace,' and he stood swaying with anger as he warded off his mother with a flourish of his hand.

Nur just lay bewildered on the bed, dazed by his father's outburst, incapable of realising the full force of the Chaudhri's anger, as if all his nervous energy were exhausted and he were completely unaffected by, indifferent to, things, except that his legs were shaking.

'Why don't you speak?' the Chaudhri, rushing to the bed of his son, said, now tenderly.

'Oh! forgive me, father, forgive me,' Nur hissed, sinking farther and farther away from the reach of his father's hand trembling and shaking and with the light of an abject terror in his eyes... 'Oh, forgive me, forgive me ...'

'Is this the fruit of all my labour for you?' the Chaudhri said alternately glistening with rage and patting Nur's forehead.

For the slightest moment, everything was still. Then the old woman began to soothe her son's form with her wrinkled fingers, saying, 'Calm, yourself, child, calm yourself, he is ill...'

'What has he done for the money I spent on his education?' the Chaudhri shouted, his face twisting with impatience. 'What has he done, except spoil my *izzat!* Is this the reward I get for bringing him into the world, for looking after him, educating him! Why can't God give me death and rid me of the affliction?'

As he stood there, however, his eyes fell on his son's frightened bent head, and he ground his teeth with a revulsion against himself, and wished he could take the boy in his arms, but he felt the slightest gesture on his part would send the boy away from him and he had been too hardened since the day when Nur was a child to bend his body and touch his son to communicate the remorse he now felt. 'Give him some food, mother,' he with a heavy heart and extricating himself from his mother's grasp rushed down the stairs, saying, 'Give him some essence of chicken...'

'Wait my son, wait child,' said the old woman hobbling after him. 'Son, you haven't eaten anything yourself...'

But the Chaudhri had gone stamping down the stairs and was out of reach of her entreaties and prayers.

'And now, now,' the old woman wailed. 'He hasn't even eaten a crust of bread, and he went to work at dawn on an empty stomach... *Hai...* what shall I do?' And she waited near the door of the stairs, torn between following him and coming to Nur. Then she returned towards Nur, who was slipping back into bed, pale and hushed, and stretching her arms said: 'Don't take any notice of what he says, my son; he is worried on account of you and overwrought, and he loses his temper... I am sure he is sorry at heart, and he loves you... And now he will be hungry. But never mind, I shall get you your soup and take his meal to the shop for him...'

She shambled and shuffled and hurried upstairs.

Nur lay still petrified and looking on through misty eyes at the broad naked heat of the sun. His mind seemed to be closed. Only, there was a dry taste at the base of his tongue, a parched feeling in his throat, mixed with a vague sense of betrayal. His face which had changed colour so often since the visit of the Doctor was set in a livid mould as if it were plastered with a mud mask. His brain wheeled dizzily, and he moved his head this side and that, as if he wanted to stir it into thought... But his eyes just stared hard into the air and he could not notice a thing in the crowded room...

Then, after a moment, he felt a weight rise from his belly to his chest, and stand there pressing down on his ribs. He breathed hard and turned on his side and, twisting his body, moaned as if to summon all the fragile cells of his body to come and look at the new wound that his father's hard words had inflicted on him. But he felt an increasing weakness in his legs and thought he was fainting. His limbs seemed like loose streamers falling away from his leaden trunk. The drowsy shade of the room in which he lay seemed to exaggerate his contours, and he felt as if he were breaking. His will relaxed and weakened...

And yet the bitterness of his father's cruelty lingered... This was the man... this was the man who was responsible for his very existence, this was the man who had loved him so when he was a little child in arms, with dark eyes and a fair complexion, when he was full of mischief and learning to toddle and speak... It seemed strange and unbearably tender; but his earliest memory, almost his first vivid recollection, was the Chaudhri laughing heartily as he flung him into the air playfully and kissed him at each fall, fairly smothering his face with kisses... After that, except now and then during the years, he had only worn a serious expression on his round, rugged face... But he had been proud even then of his father's hefty, handsome form. Only afraid, so afraid, that he remembered only a very few occasions when he had lifted his eyes to face him... Although he must admit, he was also attracted by the magnetic presence of the man; in fact, the war between these two emotions in him had always led to awkward collisions, and he had faltered, stumbled, stammered, perspired whenever he had to say anything to the Chaudhri... His father had towered over him, simple and stubbornly upright... Was it because of his mother's death that this difference had arisen between them? Anyhow, it was unfair... Was it because I, an only son, had been the cause of anxiety to him... I am a failure indeed... But why, oh why did he have to drag me into the dust by educating me? How could a parent expect to get a return for the money he had spent on his child? Why should he have expected anything? You produced me for your own pleasure... You produced me for your own pleasure, do you hear, and you didn't consult me beforehand! Why didn't you...? If you had to hate me... And tell me afterwards... Why did you? I didn't want to be born...

He felt his soul rising in revolt and he rolled in a frenzy. His eyes saw the injustice of it all and welled with tears.

'Oh God, why did he produce me if he had to be so hard to me? Oh, why did he have to educate me, why did he not let me sit at the shop and follow his own profession...? Oh why did he, why did he, why did he...? Why did he insist on my passing my MA if he had to blame me for it afterwards...? Oh why did he drag me...?'

No one seemed to hear his cries and in order not to waste his suffering on the empty air, he stifled his moans and with averted eyes still filled with tears, thought of the injustice more coolly.

'Whose fault is it? He gave me all this education to flatter his own vanity and not because he meant me to learn anything. And was it my fault that I couldn't get into any of the Services? Was it not because I was his son, the confectioner's son, who couldn't get any recommendations? For had I not always worked hard and always been top of my class? Of course, he couldn't understand what books or anything meant. But had I not always passed in the first division? Did he not hate me because, not having flourished himself, he could not see his own son fail to ascend the pinnacles of glory so that he could call the faithful to come and witness the success of his investment... And he hit me...'

His tears ran down his cheeks and he was convulsed with sobs... 'He has worked so hard in the grime and the dirt of the shop, the wretch has become surly and bad tempered serving his impatient customers,' he thought. 'But it was swinish the way he treated me, keeping a strict watch on everything I did. I must return home at seven. I must not consort with this man and that man. I must be respectful to his friends, his trusted friends, the pious practitioners of five prayers a day, who were always trying to kiss me and asking me to come and sit on their laps... And I dared not complain because they threatened to tell him that I didn't go to say prayers at the mosque regularly... What right had he to fill me with fear... It was fear that had kept me from telling him openly about things... fear and his ignorance, for how could I have explained to him that Darwin said there wasn't a God, and Huxley was an agnostic... What was Darwin to him and who was Huxley?...'

But he felt he was being naive, thinking like that... Only the blows rankled.

'Oh! God, oh! My God... Oh! My mother, my mother, come and take me... I am burning, I am bursting, I am torn... Oh come, they have crushed me, they have ruined me, they have broken me, they have made me ill, they have destroyed me, your son, and there is none in this hovel, there is none who loves me at all... Oh, I was an orphan, my mother, I was an uncared for orphan when you died... Why, oh why did you have to bring me into the world if you had to leave me...? Oh why did he have to have me if he had to loathe the very sight of me...? Why did he have to do that, why...' But he couldn't go on. His cries were becoming louder and the reiterated hiccups of his sobs were choking him so that he would have to shriek to be heard even by his own ears. And he didn't want the women upstairs to come down, because he would be too ashamed to face anyone. And yet he could not control the passion that he had let loose in himself, the anger, the resentment, the grief and the longing that lay choking him now...

He turned on his side and suddenly, his whole form was numbed, as if he had been struck in the heart.

For a moment he writhed in a paroxysm. The frenzied fire in his head drummed through his temples, the hot tears of remorse ran from his eyes, and his hard teeth ground a swooning sigh.

His throat suddenly brought up a profusion of saliva rich with blood and he lurched over to throw it into the spittoon.

He kept his head hanging over the streaks of dribbling blood and gaped weakly into the spittoon for a confirmation of his dread. The streaks of blood clotted the edge of the brass bowl. There was a coloured space before his eyes. He was sure now...

'O mother,' he cried and clutched the sheet tight. His brain was faint, the light of his eyes dimming slowly like an invisible anguish and his mind blended in a soundless void. He opened his mouth to call his grandma. But he felt the nerves of his body relaxing, as if the pain were being pressed out by the inexorable advance of death... 'Nur, my child, Nur, wake up and drink this essence,' his grandmother said, coming towards the bed... 'Nur...'

His face looked strange.

She stood fixed to the ground. Then she struggled on heavy feet to the bed and shook him with trembling fingers, calling the while, 'Nur, Nur, Nur my son, awake...'

But his face turned... and hung limply aside...

'Hai, hai!' she lifted her voice and cried. *'Hai hai! Hai hai!'* And she struck the palms of her hands on her breasts, on her forehead,

on her face and moaned and howled and tore her hair as she fell across his neck.

The women on the top storey came screaming down, beating their breasts, their thighs, their foreheads, their cheeks and their breasts again and cried, *'Hai, hai! Hai hai! Hai hai!'*

The women of the neighbourhood rushed and, entering the room, began to beat their bodies deliberately crying and wailing, *'Hai hai! Hai hai!'*

The body of death lingered on the sick bed.

Death of a Hero

Epitaph for Maqbool Sherwani

Death of a Hero

Epitaph for Maqbool Sherwani

The poplars whirred past him... And they still came towards him, on both sides of the road... Long unending lines of poplars...

But when he thought about it he found that it was actually he who was whirring past them on his motor-bike.

The leaves of the trees had been much more green two days ago, when he had fled from Baramula to Srinagar, than they were now in the light of the declining sun, while he was returning from Srinagar back to Baramula.

'Perhaps,' he said to himself in the diffused language of the wordless colloquy within him, 'perhaps, I fancy the leaves were much more green because the autumn is a sad season in our land.'

'Or perhaps it is the sunset...'

'Also death — the death of those whom the invaders had murdered!... And fear for oneself!...'

And he became conscious of his increasingly morbid preoccupation with the poet's lament, which was forming on his tongue without becoming fluid, the lament about the possibility of his own death...

As the rutted, straight tarmac road dissolved under the wheels of his 'Triumph', he had another fateful echo augury in his mind from the days of his childhood in the convent school, the Biblical phrase: 'How sweet for our souls to be borne to the skies, our journey done, our journey done...'

But he felt afraid of the potency of the phrase if it should apply to himself. He looked away.

The wintry sky on this late afternoon, the red sun tinting the snowy clouds above the mountains, and the chill mist covering the shallows and the swamps of the threatened valley, all seemed to bring the shadows nearer. The front was only ten or twelve miles away and yet it was as quiet as in the peaceful village in the middle of the valley.

'*La hol billah!*' he mumbled the cautionary phrase to calm himself.

He recalled that he had gone through so many emotions during the last three days: the feeling of weakness during the flight from his little home town after the Pakistani raiders had occupied it, the fear that he might not get to Srinagar, the elation of being in that odd room with the others in Amira Kadal, the shock of finding out that those who had begun this sudden invasion, with loot as soon as they arrived in the villages, were the so called 'Muslim brethren', the utter frustration of the confusion which prevailed in the city, then the mixed exaltation and fear of being chosen to go back to Baramula to rally the people, and, underneath it all, the complete innocence about what would happen to him if the tribesmen were already there... But there was, below the surface, a feeling he did not wish to acknowledge, the sense of chivalry: against tribalism — the genuine human response of pity.

And now, this was more boring than ever, this ride back home, because he could not even think in the state of emotional stress, did not know his destination, or the way to get there if the road was blocked...

The noise of the machine dispelled his confusion, even as it sent the sparrows in the poplars scattering into the chenars in the fields by the road. Only the sights and sounds of the evening landscape filled his senses: bleak, dreary uncultivated fields with the stubbles of the last harvest, the melancholy willows leaning over small pools, the pine forests on the slopes of the mountain, weighted down by dark, ominous clouds on the right above Gulmarg, and the peaks of the mountain ranges standing steel grey in the distance.

There was not a soul stirring on the landscape on either side of him...

Instinctively, he jerked his head up, against fear, as though to rise above the natural humility of his being before reality.

And he decided in his private colloquy that he must go on, once he had decided to go... Things were badly mixed up. But he must go right ahead and not be craven and panicky and confused any more. He was going to Baramula, perhaps to certain death. But the head of the volunteer corps had said to him: 'Maqbool Sherwani — we are in peril! We must do everything we can to avert the disaster! We must save our people! We must stand by them and each other... We must resist the butchery with our bare hands...' Apart from other things, it was the horror of the butchery which had moved him, and his advance into danger became a kind of protest against occupation of Baramula by the raiders.

Somewhere between the impact of these words and his own uneasiness, lay the fear; somewhere, under his skin, in the nerves above the tendons and the sinews of his body, there were uncontrolled tremors, as though the taut muscles were relaxing, and accepting the choice he had made.

Neither he nor his people had provoked this onslaught. And yet they were being punished. But to the poet in him, this seemed always to be so, Allah notwithstanding...

The situation had arisen all in three days, in which every Kashmiri would be tested. Those who believed in God would accept their fate as though it was the trial on judgement day. But those who hoped for a new morning for Kashmir would have to fight because only through survival would there be a chance to metamorphose the thoughts, opinions and beliefs of the young from the past servility. In such a strange situation, he told himself, the only thing to do was to go on, like a sleepwalker, to transcend the occasion, as though inspired...

Lest his naive resolve seems too heroic to himself, he relaxed the stance of his head from the rigid inclination to the left and looked on to the right.

The rice fields of Pattan were showing up now, tiers of lush green, yellowed here and there by the setting sun where paddy was ripe for cutting. The world of nature engulfed his ardent young poet's spirit. His fondness for the lush vegetation and flowers of Kashmir had always been the nostalgia of a man living with poor arid souls, the hightening produced by the lovely gardens and falling waters as an escape from his own burning heart. And soon the big village itself stood before him with its wooden houses. He knew it to be as shaky and ramshackle and decaying as Baramula, and dirty, with garbage dumps and smelly little rivulets of drains in the gulleys, but it looked, at this distance, like the picturesque villages of Switzerland, such as the nuns had shown him at school in their photograph albums. The groups of chenar trees on the outskirts, looked purple and gold and turquoise in the departing light.

Now he could see a few dim figures crouching by the putrid pond, seemingly women fetching water.

And soon a shepherd was leading his goats and sheep with uplifted stick by the willows on the right hand side of the road.

But the rows of the straggling roadside shops, on the half a mile or so before Pattan; were closed, and the congeries of Kashmiris, who usually sat huddled in their cloaks smoking the common hookah, were absent.

This general emptiness betokened the spreading fear of the Almighty, or perhaps, worse still, the actual occupation by the raiders.

A drowsy mongrel dog woke up from under the boards of a wayside stall and yelped at the motorcycle.

He slowed down the engine, which backfired noisily and made the dog run abreast of the machine and bark more viciously. This seemed like the proverbial warning from hell — as it sent shivers through his weakening legs.

He decided to pull up by Mahmdoo's cookshop, which stood about a hundred yards outside Pattan. If anyone could give him the news, it was Mahmdoo.

But the noise of the motorcycle may create panic. He shut off the engine and free-wheeled along.

The dog snarled away, back to its shelter...

~

The door of Mahmdoo's cookshop was closed. But from the chinks in the rough wooden boards, Maqbool could see a cotton wick earthen saucer lamp lighting the gloom.

'Mahmdoo,' he whispered.

There was no response. Only the flickering light glowed.

'Oh Mahmdoo, Hatto! ...It is me — Maqbool Sherwani!'

With his eyes more accustomed to the gloom, as they rivetted into the interior through the chinks, he could now see the huge platform above the earthen oven on which Mahmdoo usually sat, baking hot bread, or stirring the various meats in the cauldrons, or brewing salt tea from the brass *samovar.*

Obviously, Mahmdoo had not been cooking.

Maqbool surmised that the shrewd cookshop-keeper had accounted discretion the better part of valour, for the place where food was to be had would be one of the first to be visited by the hungry invaders. At least that had been so in the half of Baramula which the raiders had taken before he left... Did this mean that Pattan had been occupied? But there would have been Pakistani sentries all over the place, and certainly on the main road, if they had already reached here...

'Mahmdoo!' he called again.

Not from inside the shops, but, from behind him, across the road, came a whisper: 'Come this side.'

Maqbool turned round and saw Gula, the young son and assistant of Mahmdoo, in his own tunic and salwar, standing by his motorcycle.

'Father is in the sitting room of Pandit Janki Nath,' Gula said. 'He would like you to come there. But, he says, hide the motorcycle somewhere before you come ...Shall I take it to the back of the shop...'

'No, it is heavy and you will fall with it,' Maqbool said. 'I shall wheel it there and hide it, if you show me the way.'

Gula, excited at the prospect of being able to handle the motorcycle after Maqbool would go up to see his father, went ahead into the alleyway eagerly enough.

The alley was narrow and the energy and the concentration required to manouevre the heavy machine up to the doorway of the courtyard brought sweat to his face. Fortunately, the space outside the backdoor was wider. And he negotiated the cycle into the small courtyard, full of pitchers and dirty utensils and fuel and all the other muck of the cookshop.

'Don't you tinker with the machine!' he said to Gula with an affectionate smile. 'The motor has a habit of running away.'

The boy who had been itching to handle the machine, docilely followed Maqbool to where his father sat in Pandit Janki Nath Kaul's room.

Mahmdoo got up cordially and shook the right hand of Maqbool with both his puffy hands.

'Hatto, you have grown fatter with doing nothing!' Maqbool greeted him. 'And you are beaming with happiness! Have you been eating up all the food in your cookshop yourself?'

'Maqbool!' Mahmdoo protested at the banter and apologised: 'I can't help my fat body. You know — the oil and butter get into one's skin when one's cooking!...'

'What is the news?'

'Please do sit down, sire.'

'A wonderful carpet and cushions! How did the Pandit trust you not to make them greasy?'

'Sire, when it is a question of life and death, even a money-lender like Pandit Janki Nath can forge about his property... You are a learned man and don't know much about the ways of men. They fled to Srinagar three days ago after they received the news of the death of three relations in Baramula, a little while after you left...'

Maqbool searched Mahmdoo's face. The cookshop keeper obviously thought him to be a useless, unpractical fellow. Perhaps that was true, Maqbool admitted, because he had always seemed so unsure about everything to people. But was there also the insinuation that he was weak like Janki Nath?

'You had your own reasons for going to Srinagar, Maqbool Sahib, but they were protecting their skins!...' Mahmdoo said to confirm Maqbool's prognostications.

'Mahmdoo, no one is better than another in the face of death... If I am to confess the truth, I also ran away. And it needed some persuasion to bring me back...'

Against such truthfulness, Mahmdoo could only be silent. And, after a while, he also mustered the necessary courage to speak of his own fears:

'I have closed the shop, because the Pakistanis may be here any moment. And they will be hungry and will not spare me... Some half a dozen of them have already arrived at the Baramula end of this town and are staying at the Pattan house of Sardar Muhammad Jilani of Baramula... Now, when will they send us help from Srinagar?...'

Maqbool stared vacantly in front of him for a moment. He was unnerved by the news of the nearness of the raiders. And he wondered how to explain the position to Mahmdoo without causing him to panic.

'Our people are busy ... Strange ... I have never seen a Sarkar run like this. They work from a room on top of the Palladium cinema. There they sit and talk, old and young. The wiser heads debate ... The young men have formed an army and have collected all kinds of arms. Jawaharlal has condemned Pakistan for helping the Pattan raiders to attack Kashmir...'

'Then we are totally against Pakistan?' Mahmdoo asked.

'To be sure!' answered Maqbool a trifle impatient. 'These are not Muslim brethren, who have come attacking us! If they were brothers, they should have talked to us — not begun to murder us!'

'Sire, far be it from me to suggest anything else, but you know the bazaar gossip...'

'To be sure we tried to tell Jinnah to keep off Kashmir. But the exalted butchers, and the white skins behind them, have prepared the invasion. They trained the tribesmen under Pakistani officers. They armed them and sent them in army trucks. They have set up an 'Azad Kashmir' Government in Rawalpindi, with Muhammad Ibrahim at the head. And they now say we are with them!!!'

Mahmdoo was silent again. The political words of Maqbool Sherwani were too clear to allow him to doubt, though he could not comprehend everything.

'Do you realise what they have done in Baramula? These "Muslim brothers"! In their holy war?' continued Maqbool. 'They have looted both Hindus and Muslims... And they took the shame of the women!... They may soon do the same in Pattan!...'

'As Baramula is richer then Pattan, perhaps it will take a few days for them to collect all the loot!' said Mahmdoo half from wishfulfilment and half out of bitter humour.

'But we can't sit here talking,' said Maqbool suddenly. 'I must go ahead...'

Mahmdoo dared to look up at Maqbool's face. It was a lean pale face, with the delicate golden broom of youthful fine hair on the upper lip. At once the intelligence of the young man was obvious to the shrewd shopkeeper, but, at the same time, the impetuosity and the lack of mature judgment.

'Sire, one does not walk into a burning fire,' counselled Mahmdoo. 'One allows the flames to die down a little...'

'But if one makes no effort to extinguish the fire it has a way of spreading,' said Maqbool. 'Pattan is not far from Baramula... And, after Pattan, Srinagar is not much further! And they may spread out if they are not stopped at Baramula...'

Mahmdoo could not understand how they were to be stopped at Baramula. Apart from the traditional fatalism of the villager, who had accepted all kinds of tyranny as the inevitable punishment of the poor as the evidence of his guilt in the eyes of Allah there was the commonsense cunning of the shopkeeper, which was proof against the literate. On the other hand, the Pakistanis were ruffians to send the tribals here, eating up all the chickens. He had heard that there was not one chicken left in Baramula...

'Sire...' Mahmdoo began but could not finish his sentence.

Maqbool understood the man's meaning from the curious intonation of his voice and the pallor on his face.

'I will go now, Mahmdoo,' he said. 'I will have to leave my motorcycle here...'

This sentence brought a glow on the face of Gula, though it seemed to confuse Mahmdoo.

'But you must have some warm tea,' Mahmdoo said heightening with the feeling of traditional hospitality due to a man, in the cold and the dark. 'Gul, go and make some tea...'

Maqbool would have refused if he had not suddenly become possessed with the sense of his failure with Mahmdoo. What was the use of his going to Baramula to rally people, if he could not convince this man? He sat silent with a bent head seriousness, which compelled Mahmdoo to sympathy.

'Oh! Gul, hurry, son!' Mahmdoo shouted after his son.

'The *samovar* is nearly boiling, Father,' Gula said. 'And Babu Ishaq is brewing the tea.'

Mahmdoo's face suddenly fell as a fat man's face seldom falls.

~

'Ishaq is — that teacher — once a colleague of mine — in the school at Baramula?' Maqbool asked after a while.

Mahmdoo nodded his head and then after a tense silence said: 'Never trust a cockeyed fellow!...'

Hardly had he declared this dictum when Ishaq appeared at the door, a pale, shrivelled up man, cockeyed and, therefore, lacking in the dignity of weakness which somehow surrounds everyone in the village.

'The boy won't take any lessons,' said Mahmdoo going up to him by the door in an attempt to put him off the scent and to see if he would go away. 'Gula thinks it is all a holiday...'

Mahmdoo had never been known to be inhospitable. In fact, his cookshop kept an open-door policy and many, who could not afford to buy food, came there and ate without paying. The teacher almost lived on Mahmdoo eating in lieu of the tuitions he gave to Gula.

As he sensed the coldness in Mahmdoo's voice, Ishaq felt that there was some special reason for his words. This made him explore the room. And with his uncanny squint eye, he saw Maqbool Sherwani sitting there.

Extending his right arm to wish Mahmdoo out of his way, he advanced, taciturn and paler than usual towards the stranger. And, with a pat of bonhomie, he uttered a loud greeting: 'Say Maqbool Sahib — have your leaders accepted defeat yet or not?'

Maqbool knew this school teacher to be a fanatical pro-Pakistani.

With an affected air of casual indifference, he answered: 'Come Ishaq Sahib, come...'

Ishaq came and sat down, followed by Mahmdoo whose padded face reflected the worst fears after these men had come face to face with each other.

'Our brethren from Pakistan have completely liberated Baramula,' Ishaq began challengingly. 'And they have spread out in two flanks towards Srinagar. I hear they are attacking the main town from the aerodrome side on the one hand and from Gandarbal side on the other. They have taken the Electric Power house. Srinagar is in darkness tonight. And we expect them to be in Pattan tonight or tomorrow morning.'

'Babu Ishaq, how do you know all this?' Mahmdoo asked, partly because he did not believe that Ishaq could know and partly out of pity for Maqbool Sherwani whose moral would surely break down after this talk.

'Our brothers, in the holy war, have trust in me,' said Ishaq almost in a whispered undertone. 'I did not come to teach Gula. I came to ask you to prepare food for them. Sardar Muhammad Jilani has sent orders that everything be done to welcome them when they arrive in Pattan...' And then, turning his gaze towards Maqbool without seeming to turn that way, he said: 'Deign to join our reception committee, Maqbool Sahib. You will see that your leaders will also accept the inevitable.'

'Never!' answered Maqbool. 'It is a question of principle. Do we believe in Kashmir first, or religion first?'

'In religion — in the religion of our Prophet, (may peace be upon his soul), and of our holy Koran.'

'And when did the Prophet, or the Koran, say that brother must kill brother...'

'It is not true that our brothers have done this,' said Ishaq in a shrill voice.

'Babu Ishaq,' put in Mahmdoo. 'But there are rumours from Baramula...'

'And they murdered the troops of General Rajinder Singh, whom they took prisoner at Uri, to a man!' put in Maqbool.

'Against infidels in a holy war, there is no avail!' Ishaq said showing his yellow teeth. 'Have not the Hindu Maharaja, and the Dogras crushed us all this time? We cannot surely join with the Hindus in the defence of Kashmir against our own kith and kin!'

'Against murder — one must join even with Shaitan,' said Mahmdoo with his uncanny wisdom.

'And you people talk of principles,' taunted Ishaq.

'Maqbool Sahib does not say what I say,' said Mahmdoo defending the silent guest.

'Then why does not the worthy Maqbool Sherwani answer?' insisted Ishaq.

'I have seen the raiders in Baramula with my own eyes,' said Maqbool in a husky whisper... 'Besides, I am for Kashmir. Not for its usurpation by force, but for its freedom to choose where it wants to go. And Nehru can be trusted more than Jinnah. In Karachi they still rely on foreign friends and...'

'These are lies,' said Ishaq, shaking like the branch of a willow tree. 'And your life will not be safe if you talk like this...'

'Babu Ishaq!' shouted Mahmdoo. 'Maqbool Sahib is my guest.'

'As for you, greasy cookshop-keeper!' snarled Ishaq. 'I shall see about you!...' And saying this, he got up and turned towards the door with a peculiar alacrity, nearly running into Gula who was bringing the tea tray.

The boy came and, placing the tray on the floor, began to cry.

'You know your school teacher gets angry very quickly, because he is so thin,' Mahmdoo said to console his son.

Maqbool patted Gula on the head and then said to his host: 'I have brought you trouble.'

'I will bring all the troubles you have brought me, as well as mine own to you,' he said with a slightly forced humour. 'I and Gula will have to come with you to Baramula now!' He paused for a brief moment to explore Maqbool's face for reassurance, and then began: 'I know a track through the fields. And once we reach the outskirts of Baramula, in the dark we can walk to the house of Juma, the baker... He is my cousin... Now drink up the hot tea and let's go. That snake may crawl back here...'

~

The cold frosty air of the late October night had been thickened by the smoke of burning wooden houses as Maqbool and his two companions pushed with aching feet towards a small haystack about half a mile or so out of Baramula.

For nearly four hours they had struggled forward, through the mud and the slush of the fields. And Maqbool looked haggard and worn with the strain of walking in such terrain with Mahmdoo and Gula. Because, though the talk of Ishaq had converted Mahmdoo from the shopkeeper cynic to the side of the innocents, nothing could eradicate the deep fears aroused in him, by Ishaq's fateful announcements about the expected attack on Pattan by the 'Brethren'. Mahmdoo would mistake every bush to be a tribesman and every heightened beat of the reverberating crickets in the wet fields for machine gun fire. Gula was sleepy and had to be carried in turn by Maqbool and Mahmdoo.

Maqbool too had felt, during this journey into the unknown that, at any moment, they may come across sentinels or the advance guard of the raiders; for he too had been affected by Ishaq's words. But he surmised that if they had encircled Pattan, they would already have got them, even though he and Mahmdoo had come through a circuitous path in the fields.

What had actually happened in Baramula since he left he did not know. Perhaps they were under good military leadership. And they were waiting for reinforcements before proceeding further. Or they were cautiously fanning out on the flanks of Srinagar from strategic points, as Ishaq had suggested, to probe the situation and then to attack the capital with full force. If the miracle happened, which everyone in Srinagar hoped for, and the Indian army arrived, then the situation may be saved. Otherwise...

~

He felt a certain pity for the poor cookshop-keeper and his son, to be coming with him on this desperate expedition. Some kind of decision was necessary now about these two.

'I am hungry, Father,' Gula whined even as he crumpled up and lay down at the foot of the haystack.

'Keep quiet, Hatto, be a man!' Mahmdoo rubuked him.

That gave Maqbool a cue. For a moment, he stood there listening to the audible darkness, replete with the sounds of vegetation and distant human voices. It seemed to him as though, with the exhaustion, the weight of his body had increased. He sat down and began to speak, before Mahmdoo may have the chance to say anything:

'So far we have been lucky, Mahmdoo. And I am grateful for this. I would not have liked anything to happen to you and Gula on the way, as you chose to come with me rather than stay in Pattan. Now I cannot ask you to endanger your lives any more...'

'But what are you saying?' protested Mahmdoo. 'I would rather be with you than cooking for the raiders all night under Babu Ishaq's orders!... And, after I took sides with you, he would surely have betrayed me to the murderers. You don't know Ishaq! He believes he is a great man, because he is a school teacher...'

The warm breath issued out of Mahmdoo's mouth in wisps of smoke as he sat by Maqbool and spoke these words. And his peculiar devotion, born through the chivalry of the host, which had made Mahmdoo come so far, overflowed into space. Maqbool was sure that though he could not see the face of his companion, there would be tears in the cook's eyes. He would feel lonely, when the father and son would leave him, as he had now decided they must, but the wheel of time was turning in his brain and he felt he must turn with it.

'You came with me!' he began in a gentle whisper, 'because my presence with you forced you to take my side in the argument with Ishaq. You would have cooked for Ishaq and his friends out of sheer necessity. I cannot expect you to face possible death for something you may not understand. Perhaps, tomorrow, after you have been in Baramula, you may know what I mean. Even I ran away to Srinagar, thinking everything was lost in Baramula. But I have come back, because I believe help will come to us. I do not want you to stay with me tonight —'

'Sire!' Mahmdoo protested.

'No, if you believe in me, you will have to obey my orders,' said Maqbool sharply. 'You can do something for me. By then you will have time to think and become stranger in your faith. You take Gula to Juma's house. In the morning, if you think the road is clear, send Gula to me here with a message... This plan has to be carried out. Otherwise, all three of us will die a needless death...'

Mahmdoo had no words against this logic. Besides, the suggestion to go met the curve of his own inner desire for safety. Maqbool had guessed rightly.

'I would like to sleep here by Gula — but if you say I must go, I will go...' Mahmdoo said by way of apology.

'If anything happens to me,' Maqbool said, 'Gula can take that motorcycle I have left behind your shop. The locksmith's son in Baramula will teach him how to ride it...'

'What inauspicious talk you do!' protested Mahmdoo.

'Go then —'

Mahmdoo tried to lift his son Gula in his arms. The boy was heavy. So Maqbool got up and, raising Gula from the hay bed, put him silently on Mahmdoo's back like a sack. Having once been a coolie, Mahmdoo could carry the weight easier that way.

'May Allah be with you,' Mahmdoo mumbled.

'Send Gula if you can in the morning,' Maqbool repeated his request. And, as the man walked away slowly, he began to scoop out some hay from the stack before making a cave for himself.

As soon as he lay down anyhow, he was filled with warmth for Mahmdoo, who had put himself into this awkward situation through the old Kashmiri sense of chivalry.

~

The hay had been piled up very compactly. He found that the bushels he had detached were only four feet long. And he was uncomfortable as he lay curled up like a baby. So he took another two bushels out from the side.

For a little while, he felt too desolate to go to sleep. It was strange that now, after the heat of the walk had died down in his body, he began to miss the presence of Mahmdoo and Gula and felt lonely — a kind of emptiness tinged with an endless series of anxieties, vague and amorphous, like menacing shadows cast by the captors of Baramula.

But, outside, the wind rushed through the poplars with a cold swish. Instinctively he clung to himself and pillowed his head with his left arm. Now he felt snug and calm and lay listening to the breeze and to the wetness of the earth sucking up its own moisture. And the fatigue of his body rose like the smell of country liquor to his head and closed his eyes, dissolving his heavy body into the small space around him, and starting off a series of nightmares in his head.

~

A lengthy exchange of distant rifle and machine gun fire aroused him from the crazed sleep, in which the last broken edges of dreams showed Mahmdoo and Gula as stags goring him with their horns. He lifted his head and listened, stifling the sentiments about Mahmdoo with a deliberate prejudice in favour of the fat shopkeeper. The distant rat-tat-tat of the machine gun increased. And he was filled with the forebodings which had obsessed him all the way from Srinagar. The only machine guns would be in the hands of the Pakistanis, for he had seen the abject dump of crude single-barrelled and double-barrelled rifles which the people's militia had shown him in the store rooms of the Palladium cinema. But the well equipped Indian army may have come...

He took a deep breath and listened more intently to locate the exact direction where the sound of firing came from. It was on the Gandarbal side of Baramula. Perhaps the raiders were about to attack Srinagar from that flank, in force. Not that he knew anything about how armies fought, but it seemed strange to his youthful mind that they could advance so far on the flanks, leaving their middle undefended. For if an army had moved with him from

Srinagar, on or near the main road to Baramula, it could have got behind them in Gandarbal through the tracks from Pattan and cut them off. But they were no fools, the men who had organised this invasion, Generals Gracey and Tariq. And Liaqat and Abdul Qayum Khan dare not have a defeat on their hands, for Jinnah wanted a *fait accompli,* the possession of Kashmir, knowing he could tackle all the moral hullabaloo, of the United Nations afterwards. Dr. Taseer, who had come once to persuade Kashmir to accept the blood brotherhood, but who had found them recalcitrant, had said at last with ruthless logic: 'He who has the big stick will have the buffalo!...'

If the fighting was on, he must get us and go and do something. He had no right to rest here. If he had any courage, he must be in the fray now...

But what exactly could he do? He could only sound opinion, tell them the news of imminent help from India and wait.

He wondered what the Russian guerillas had done in similar circumstances under Hitler's occupation? Or the people of the French resistance? And now he regretted that he had only heard rumours of what had happened in the war and had read no books. Never had he felt so abject at his lacks as now. Still he knew that this sudden descent of murder on his land was not an act of God, but a planned brutality to cow people down to submit, and resistance to it was the only virtue. Later he must ask questions and learn the things, so necessary for a young poet. He could not even afford the fare to go to a poetical festival in Srinagar, when he was at school before the world war years. His father had been angry, because he could not give him the money he had asked for, and his mother and sister had been giving him cash from their small savings... And yet his spirit (or was it ambition?) demanded more and more until he had begun to believe that he was one of the most selfish men around Baramula. And the torment of this guilt had made him try to cultivate humility for its own sake, and he had drowned himself in political work. Reading the poems of Faiz, Majrooh Jafri, Sahir, Nadim, from borrowed books. They had certainly heightened his emotions to a pitch. And this was truly romantic. But why were they not in Kashmir? — Except Nadim...

The rifle fire was sustained. And he felt he could not enjoy the luxury of self-pity any more. He must in the absence of any other concrete plans, go and reconnoitre the position in Baramula. The cover, which the darkness afforded, would help him. Only Gula would not find him here, if he came in the morning with a message from Mahmdoo; but he knew that the shrewd Mahmdoo would understand. So he crawled out of the haystack and began to shake off the straw from his clothes.

~

The snow flakes which had obviously fallen during the night seemed to have melted and the land was slushy as he began to trudge in the diminishing pitch dark before twilight. A sharp wind blew and cut through his woollen jacket. He gathered his muffler around his neck and felt like a scarecrow walking along. That was an advantage, because in case he was observed he could just stand and stretch his hands out, though the tribesmen were more sharp-eyed than he gave them credit for...

Now that he was going along he wanted to make certain where he was going.

The smoke, which still arose from the middle of the town decided him: It would be futile to plunge into Baramula just like that. He must keep afloat on the sea of existence. And, for this reason, it was best for the while, not to yield to the longing for home, but to attend to the bigger anxiety and avoid being caught.

A shiver went down his spine as he realised that he might walk straight into the arms of a Pakistani sentry or be picked off by a bullet from one of the hawk-eyed ones. And, again, his body and mind were in the grip of the crisis which had occupied him before he had dozed off in the haystack: Did one grow up just to be ready to be shot? What did it all mean? Where was Allah Mian? These were questions arising from fear. He sensed the tremors inside himself.

And, in this agitation, the choice before him became an obsession. He stopped for a moment, his chin uplifted and his eyes exploring an avenue, chafing at himself for his bad nerves. And then he reasoned, almost audibly: 'Fear is the natural humility of man before ugly reality!...'

A little way away from the town, he knew, stood the Presentation Convent, where people were perhaps sufficiently near to be in the know of all that had happened in the three days he had been away and sufficiently far to be out of the trouble spots. As Christians and white folk they would be immune. Besides his father's cousin, Rahti, worked as house mother in the hospital and her husband, Salaama, was the watchman of the convent.

Skirting around the fields, so that he could keep out of visible distance from the town, he headed towards an uprise from which he could descend onto the convent, without the risk of being observed.

In spite of the agitation in him, he pretended to be as matter of fact as though he had been to the fields for a walk from the convent.

As he sighted the group of buildings of the Presentation Convent, he found the main house smoking.

Footsore and weary from a further trudge after the long walk from Pattan, he felt listless.

He stopped to see things clearly, imagining that, in the deceptive darkness, he was mistaking the smoke of the chimney for fire. Perhaps it was some other building in the nearby town.

But as far as his eyes could peer into the distance, and figure things out, it was, indeed, the main convent house which was smouldering slowly, the smoke like a dense morning mist.

He tried to remain calm and absorb the shock, arguing that he did not really feel any emotion or sentiment about a holy place like a mosque, a temple or a convent. But, all the same, he realised that the raiders had sacked this place. He wondered how the Pakistani officers, who knew of the help given to them by the White generals, had allowed the burning of a missionary centre. The marauders seemed to have engulfed not only the town but also the outskirts, as the weeds in the forest engulf the shrubs and flowers.

So his plan to seek safety among the Christians had failed.

He stood for quite a while wondering what to do next, unable to believe that the Muslim brethren could set fire to a holy place. But the truth smouldered into his brain with the smoke. Clearly this incendiarism had been recently committed.

At last he was encouraged by the view of the standing houses in the convent courtyard, to push on.

~

Gingerly, he advanced towards the hospital side of the convent, in the courtyard of which Salaama and Rahti had a room.

The frost crinkled under his feet and the beautiful frozen bushes made him feel lonely.

He dared not think of danger, or imagine a catastrophe, for he knew that would be the end of him. And he feigned a casual air, deliberately toughening his sinews, tightening his face and stiffening his neck in the process. This made him a trifle theatrical, but he allowed himself this willed artificiality in the interests of morale. The decision to go forward was like crossing the rubicon from fear to courage. Pausing to look before and after, again he saw that the coast was clear. He hurtled down the hillside.

Long before he got to the courtyard of the hospital, he was challenged by the sweeper Fatah, who having asked: 'Who are you?' ran terror-stricken into the servants' quarters in the courtyard.

'Oh Hatto! It is me, Sherwani,' Maqbool said in whispers loud enough to be heard. But the diffused terror of the invaders possessed Fatah like a ghost. And he was lost to view among the babble of voices in the servants' quarters.

~

Luckily for Maqbool, Rahti looked out of the iron bars of the back window of her room and recognised him.

'It is our Maqbool,' she said to her husband Salaama, who had awakened from the late sleep into which he had fallen.

Salaama was nearly delirious and looked with bleary eyes, incomprehensively at his wife, who had been keeping a vigil by him all night.

Rahti went out and brought Maqbool in, quietly, allaying the fears of the other servants, who had come out to their doors and windows, to see if this presaged a new attack by the raiders.

'They are all scared,' Rahti began, 'that the Pakistanis might come back. And, to be sure, there is no knowing what they will do next — if the monsters return! They nearly killed him —' And as she uttered the last words her control broke down. A lump came into her throat and her eyes filled with tears.

'Uncle Salaama,' Maqbool said.

Rahti moved her head up and down affirmatively and her demure, housemother's face lit up with anguish.

'Is he badly hurt?' Maqbool asked as they got into the raised verandah of the servants' barracks.

She stopped outside the door and told him in whispers: 'They shot at him while he was guarding the front gateway. And, praise be to Allah, the bullet just grazed past his skull. But the bone was chipped and he lost nearly a pitcherful of blood. He collapsed. He had been delirious since... And the whole day, yesterday, and all night, he has been... groaning... He had just dozed off a little till your coming awakened him...'

Maqbool entered the neat little room with the big bed and came and leaned over Salaama.

'I am sick, sick...' Salaama burbled like a drunkard from a slobbering mouth which he could open with seeming difficulty: 'Sick!... And those sons of the Devil. They murdered the little mother.'

'Do not strain yourself!' Rahti cautioned him. 'I shall tell him everything!' And she turned to Maqbool. 'They killed Sister Teresaline, the Assistant Mother Superior, wounded the Mother Superior and relieved themselves in the chapel!...'

Maqbool perched on the edge of the big bed, his face covered with sweat from the terror that arose in him at this news. And he was ashamed by the truth of his prognostications. Or was it his inner timidity, he wondered. Or the humility before the terrible things.

He put his hands into Salaama's and, for a while, there was silence in the room. Then Salaama groaned and moved his head uncomfortably from side to side.

'Why have you come back to this hell?' Rahti said as she turned from where she was lighting the primus stove.

The young man paused to explore the level of his mind which had been blurred by what he saw before him. And, then, without raising his voice, so that he should not sound heroic, he said: 'We have to resist the monsters...'

Having said this, he felt that some bigger sanction than his own voice was necessary, because inside him he was even now shrinking from the final words he had left unpronouned, 'or die'. So he added: 'Our comrades in Srinagar think that... And if our luck is good, then, already as I talk, Nehru may have gone into action and sent the Indian army to our relief. The Maharaja has joined India, Srinagar was free when I left yesterday afternoon —'

'We heard different tales,' said Rahti impatiently. 'All we know is that Baramula is completely in the grip of the Pakistanis! And they are filling their trucks with loot. There is no hope here!... If only they would leave us alone now and not come back here... Salt tea — or with sugar?...' All her words were shrill except the last ones.

Maqbool felt a constriction in his throat as he tried to react to her despair. And he could not say anything. He merely sat noticing her nervous hands washing the teapot with hot water to get ready for tea. The valley seemed to him to have become an orchestra of bitter feelings of despair instead of human voices.

'If there is sugar, I will have it with sugar,' he said after all.

'Ya Allah!...' Salaama pronounced the Islamic incantation even as he turned his head from one side to the other. ...'The ache is terrible,' he said. 'Ya Allah... Forgive us. ...But crush those sons of Shaitan, the marauders!...'

Maqbool felt his pulse and knew that Salaama was running high temperature.

'Try not to speak,' Rahti said in her familiar housemother manner.

'O woman,' he burst out, 'how can I forget these sons of Iblis, when they murdered the little mother in cold blood. I want to get up and murder them all!... Maqbool, they are no good!... They have not only murdered Christians, Hindus and Sikhs, but also Muslims... And I hope Allah will punish them for this!... This woman has no faith... She neither believes in Allah nor in Shaitan!... Perhaps she believes in Yessuh Messih*...' At this he was seized with a fit of coughing and lifted his head, while Maqbool supported his back.

'But is there an Allah?' Maqbool whispered, hoping his uncle would not hear. 'Yessuh Messih was a real person and suffered for mankind — was crucified!'

'Here is some tea,' Rahti said to her husband. Her sorrow seemed to have turned into a cynical tight-mouthed hopelessness.

'I will give it to him,' Maqbool said as he took the cup from her.

This caused a tremor of tenderness to go through Rahti and she melted towards Maqbool and thus towards her husband.

'No, I will give it to him,' she said. 'You have your tea. There it is...'

Maqbool got up and yielded his place to her, so that she could help Salaama sip his tea. And, he took up the cup she had poured for him and stood sipping it, even as he looked out of the window at the mountains beyond.

The twilight was reddening, as though in anticipation of the sunrise. And for a moment he felt that nature would overwhelm the thought of the marauders in his head, even engulf the invaders.

'Our people have hearts,' Salaama said taking his mouth away from the cup. 'I wish I could get up... I would teach these ruffians the lesson of their lives!...' He coughed and nearly spilled the tea.

* Jesus Christ

'Drink up your tea first,' Rahti scolded him. 'You haven't the heart to kill a sparrow. So why boast so much! There is no choice for the poor but to suffer like Yessuh Messih...'

'O go away Hatto, go...' he said impatiently and brushed the tea cup so that it fell on the floor at Maqbool's feet. 'I am not like others who will not shout,' Salaama continued defiantly. 'I want to fight!...' And he lay back exhausted by the effort to say his say.

All three of them were silent for a while. Rahti was angry, but taciturn, with her anxiety for her husband.

'That is what the people of Srinagar are saying,' put in Maqbool, as though talking aloud to himself. 'We will not accept their rule. And we shall defend ourselves — our freedom...'

'Brave words are not bullets!' said Rahti cynically, but in a soft voice.

Maqbool came and sat by Salaama again for a while. Then he touched his hands in silence and got up.

'Don't run your head into the noose,' Rahti said. 'They must be looking for you. Stay here a while.'

'No, I must go,' said Maqbool grimly. 'I have chosen my path!'

'That path leads straight to hell!' Rahti shouted.

'Go, go Hatto, go!...' said Salaama excitedly as he raised his head again. 'Go... You will find that the heart of your uncle Salaama is in the right place still...'

'Lie back still,' Rahti ordered.

Maqbool who had stopped to hear Salaama, issued out into the courtyard.

~

The cover which the darkness had supplied for his descent upon the convent was being removed by the dawn that rose blood-red from the mountains below the eastern sky. The impetuousity that had made him emerge from the safety of Rahti's room soon gave place again to timidity. He feigned an easy natural gait, however, and headed, through a deserted plain, towards the north end of the main street of Baramula, where the big house of the landlord Sardar Muhammad Jilani stood. His head was bent, as though it was weighed down by the thoughts of Allah in a pious Muslim. But his eyes were like gaping pits, unable to believe in the desolation of the once alive Baramula.

In this heightened consciousness of the doom which had settled upon his home town, he was aware that there were two kinds of people now left, the many like Rahti who where inclined fatalistically, to accept what had happened, in spite of their detestation of the misdeeds of the Pakistanis, and the few like Salaama and himself, who were self-willed and were increasingly possessed by the feelings of protest and resistance. There may be others, he felt, who did not know anything of anything, who were merely like innocent jelly cast into the mould of daily habit and the routine life, wrapped up in the symbols of a religious negativeness, a state of benumbed spirituality or ritualistic five-prayers-a-day worship or mere family loyalty.

Suddenly, he saw some coolies of Baramula by the octroi post, bearing huge boxes and trunks and sacks into the waiting trucks, which was ostensibly the loot on the way out to Pakistan.

He must not be seen near the octroi post, because the police station was near at hand; and once seen by a policeman he, who was known to the law as a notorious rebel against the Maharaja's rule, would be done for. And yet the mansion of Sardar Muhammad Jilani was at this end of the town.

Anyhow, what guarantee was there that he would be any safer in that house, because, if the information that Babu Ishaq had given him in Pattan was correct, the big landlord of Baramula was acting as the head of the fifth column. Ghulam was at his best, a callow, spoilt child, irresponsible, weakwilled and impressionable in the extreme. It was true that he had given money for the struggle against Maharaja Hari Singh but his fear of his father may have damned up his rebellious sympathies, unless he was still under the influence of his business partner, Muratib Ali. But as against Muratib, there would be the more powerful voice of the ambitious little lawyer, Ahmed Shah, who, Maqbool had heard, had gone over to the Pakistanis. But Ghulam was also his friend, who listened to poetry.

He changed his direction back towards the convent. And, taking cover behind a broken tonga, which stood deserted in the clearing before the congested town, he tried to deliberate on his strategy.

As soon as he stopped, however, all thoughts seemed to fly away from his head, and he had left to him only a beating heart.

It was queer how, when one paused on one's way anywhere, fear seemed to become almost concrete, a kind of electric shock sent into the body by each sight and sound. He tried to stare at fear itself.

The tonga — had it been broken by the raiders? And were there any Pakistanis in the stables beyond there?

He applied his ears to listen to the possible neighing of horses, but there was a dread silence.

His loneliness gripped him, until he had to cough deliberately to relieve the tension.

He must begin to walk, but whither...

The answer came: Muratib Ali was the safest bet. Also, his own house was near Muratib's.

~

The thought of going nearer home was exciting like the prospect of Muratib's past generosity. For however shallow the opinions of this businessman, his heart could be depened upon. The thing was to get there without being challenged, or without running into someone who may recognise him. There was an approach to Muratib's house from his own lane.

But the dangerous distance to be crossed was the foot-bridge across the river to the main bazaar near his own house.

An alternative course was to get to his own lane, from the dry pond in the fields to the east of the town, by wading into the river half a mile further back on the Pattan road.

He began to walk and this activity dissolved the envoleping anxiety to an extent.

He had not gone far when cries of *'Allah ho Akbar! Allah ho Akbar!'* rent the air from the side of the octroi post.

Obviously, it was the Pakistanis. And he felt it was a wise decision on his part not to go into the main bazaar. But, perhaps, if they were concentrated in this area, he had the chance to steal across the foot-bridge across the river to his own lane.

The resonant praise of Allah repeated itself, but the tone in which it came spread an involuntary chill into his soul. It was fear in the worst sense because it made him shiver. He paused to control himself, to prevent the feeling from becoming the obsession of cowardice.

'Maqbool!...' he mumbled to himself.

A vague apprehension of the distance, through which he would have to expose himself on the open bridge came to him. In order to avoid such exposure and master his fear before it could become cowardice, he decided, on the spur of the moment, that he should go back to the haystack.

He had barely turned when he knew it was far away now.

Rahti's bicycle was the kind of vehicle which would do the trick.

And without much thought of whether Rahti would permit him to use her cycle, he began to walk back.

As he proceeded back towards the convent, absorbed in the sheer physical efforts, there was a slight disturbance among the leaves of a chenar tree. He jumped but soon heard a bird singing and realised that it was a lark who had upset him.

'Should I ask Rahti's permission to take her cycle away or should I not?' he mumbled to himself in order to avoid being jumpy and to fill the vacancy in his mind, which was in danger of being occupied by instinctive dreads. But he did not resolve the question, though he went on repeating it like a wordless incantation.

Fatah, who was on guard at the door of the courtyard, again ran shouting loudly: 'Save me, Save me!'

Maqbool ran after him, caught him and shook him, saying: 'Hatto, it is me, Maqbool!'

Fatah looked at Maqbool terror-stricken, but remained silent as though mesmerised.

Maqbool left him and got to the verandah. He found the ladies bicycle standing by the door, and he just announced: 'Rahti aunt, I am taking your bicycle away!' And he rode away without waiting for an answer.

Afterwards, he felt guilty that she might need it to go to the town to fetch something for Salaama. But knowing that the town was in the grip of those who had sacked the convent, he surmised that the machine was useless to her.

~

Once he was astride the bicycle, he seemed to feel more free. The distance from the convent to his own lane was about a mile by the detour on the outskirt of the town, half of it through the fairly safe grove of chenar trees and the other half across the footpath where the town houses ended in swamps, the pools and the puddles.

A lean dog yelped away from above the debris of fallen leaves in the grove, and, again, he was startled out of his wits. But the dog seemed more frightened of him as he ran shrieking away.

Further up, a flock of ducks whirred over the chenar trees. He looked up and saw that their wings were touched with the silver of the risen sun above the giant hills. An involuntary sigh escaped his lips at the realisation of the total misery into which this land of the poet's dreams and visions, had been suddenly plunged by the invasion. And he begun to hum the words of the old Kashmiri poet Majoor:

'O Kashmir, my beloved motherland,
    When the morning of a new life
Dawns upon the world
    Its first ray will touch your own
High and beautiful forehead!'

At the end of the grave, on a small platform by the deserted tomb of a Pir, he saw half a dozen men, raiders by the look of them, kneeling in the attitude of Sajdah prayer, their eyes closed, their faces turned towards the West.

Would they break off from their prayers to challenge him?

His heart beat fast. His face went pale. And his eyes were full of mist.

All the six men got up with hands folded before them and did not look this side or that, but perserved in their prayer.

He was safe.

It was a miracle that none of them had been walking about or sitting down, preparing for prayer. And the irony of it struck him, as he reached past the tomb, to the cover of some fishermen's huts, that these brutal men could be devoutly praying, though only the previous night, perhaps they had been looting and murdering. Or this bunch might be the more decent among the invaders!... Or perhaps they were just simple, fanatical barbarians, who really believed in the holy war, in which, they had been told, they were engaged here, and their prayers were merely automatic gestures, repeated without any understanding of the meaning of the Arabic words. This question of whether there was a God or not, had always oppressed him. The death of innocents had proved that there was no God, except that Allah might just now be looking after him.

The benefit of doubt could be given to God, because there were three small fishing boats tied to pegs by the riverside, and the stream was not too wide, as also utter silence prevailed on the road.

The chance of a safe passage across the river started a nausea in his stomach. The bile came into his mouth.

Strange that when a man resolved to do something, the remnants of weakness hidden in the body reacted against him.

He spat out the bile.

Then quickly he put the bicycle into the smallest of the boats, going back to untie the rope from the wooden peg.

'The oars! The oars! Where were the oars?'

His heart sank when he knew that the fishermen seldom left their oars behind.

Grimly, he accepted the fact that he would have to drift down, steering the boat with his hand, and hope that, before the end of the mile where the town began, he would have crossed the hundred yards or so to the other side.

The current was swift and panic seized him.

Desperately, he lowered the cycle into the river at the end of the boat and began to steer with its hulk. The wheels were like sieves, but the middle part seemed to work, tilting the boat ever so slightly in the opposite direction.

Seeing the distance that separated him from the objective, he nearly wanted to pray. But the current was strong and gave no promise that his indifferent oar would succeed. So no gratitude was due to anyone.

Resourcefully, he lowered his torso and joined his arm to the chain wheel.

This was more effective. He persisted.

The swift current helped him, though the boat was only three fourths of the way by the time it had floated down nearly half a mile.

There was nothing to do, but to lie down, keep the nearly frozen arm adjusted to the broadest part of the bicycle and steer clear of the danger.

Time seemed to become endless.

And yet a furlong before the foot-bridge his boat entered a small swampy rivulet which gave him cover. Also, there was a garbage heap across which he could climb out, with his bicycle.

As he crossed the garbage heap the bile rose in his mouth again, this time with the stink of the refuse as well as the tension inside him.

He contemplated the slithery slopes of the mound of rubbish with a deliberate will to accept them. Perhaps, it is necessary, as Islam taught, to go through the sewer before one could come clean. And he was doing so literally now. That would be the inner core of the poem, if he lived to write one. Also he must not forget even a single aspect of the squalor, now, as he had always done in his attraction towards love poetry. Like Jigar he had wanted to escape from asafoetida of his home town, the decay and the hopelessness. Perhaps, all the arid souls around him, his poor father, his mother, would appreciate the high pitch of his words now after what they had seen. And they would awaken rather than accept their fates...

He was through to the unpaved road. He quickly got astride the bicycle.

~

Just at this moment, he seemed to himself most lucid, as though his awareness had become, through the dangers that faced him, an all enveloping, comprehensive intelligence, percolating to his senses and putting them on a plane where he had a permanent and tender understanding of the causes of the decay.

The sun beat faster and faster behind his back, though the draughts which blew from the murky little lanes was chilling.

The prolonged stretch of a big puddle, under the shadow of the wooden houses, just before his lane, forced him to alight from his cycle.

As he free-wheeled the machine, he saw Juma, Qadri and Saleem Bux, the three brothers who worked in Muratib's carpet factory, looking at him from the cavernous room which they occupied on the ground floor by the vegetable field of Ala Din, the eccentric gardener. Before he could warn them, they shouted their greetings with the warm enthusiasm of complete innocence.

'Ah Maqbool!... Where have you been? They are everywhere... Have they also got to Srinagar?...'

Maqbool shushed them and nearly slipped over the edges of mud which he was negotiating. But it was of no avail. The fear crazed females of the household came out, and began to smile and shout greetings: *'Salam alaikum!'*

'Wa alaykum as-salam!' Maqbool answered softly and raised his hand to silence them.

'They looted the carpet factory, Maqbool. And then set it on fire!' the old mother of Juma, Qadri and Saleem Bux shouted. 'The sons of Eblis!... They even came here! But I gave them a bit of my mind and they went away!...'

'Mother,' he said coming up to the platform on which they all stood. 'We have to be patient...'

'Patience!' the old woman shrieked. 'They have burnt the factory from which came our living, and you ask us to be patient!... What has happened to you all?...'

'Mother!... Mother!...' her sons cautioned her 'Maqbool —'

'You are all cowards!' the old woman shouted with such force that the hens on the garbage by her doorsteps fluttered away.

'I will go and see Muratib Ali,' said Maqbool. 'Do you think he will be at home?'

'What can he do, that do-nothing!' the old woman said cynically. 'He just sat at home and allowed the factory to be looted!'

'Mother, don't make such a noise!' Juma said again. 'The Pakistanis wanted carpets for their homes!...'

'Fool, don't you see,' the old woman said cocking her left eye, 'that my voice will keep those beasts away till Maqbool can get home.'

Maqbool's face puckered into a smile as he walked away towards Muratib Ali's big house in the main street, at the end of the lane.

~

There was the old unruly drumming under his chest as Maqbool reached the sitting room of Syed Muratib Ali's house. The young factory owner was smoking the *hookah* as he sat in an English armchair, and he looked up at Maqbool with a quizzical expression, which was part pleasure, part horror. For a moment neither of them said anything, as the visitor was breathless, while the host was dazed at the sudden arrival of this nationalist partisan. Then Muratib Ali said: 'Why have you come back? To put your head in the noose?'

Maqbool did not answer, but sat down on a wicker chair opposite him, still out of breath.

'Things are terrible! You must fly from here!'

'I saw a sentry at the head of the lane. So I had to slip past him, pretending to be on business. And then I ran upstairs...'

'You seem to bear your life on the palm of your hands with a strange bravado!' Muratib said. 'Suppose the sentry had challenged you!'

'One has to take chances,' said Maqbool laconically.

'But do you realise, Maqbool brother!' Muratib began in a mildly admonishing tone.

'Our leaders have sent me,' Maqbool cut in, knowing that only the magic word 'leaders' would justify his behaviour here in the eyes of Muratib, as it had done to Mahmdoo, though there was the danger that his friend might suspect some vanity in his association of the exalted with his mission. He realised that he did feel vain from the connection, but it would be stupid if Muratib found this in him.

'The situation has gone beyond *our leaders,'* said Muratib. And then he began to puff at the hookah with a bored expression which was a cover for the terror which pervaded him. And as he looked away, his face seemed to betoken the attitude that Maqbool was not welcome.

There was a silence between them during which the gurgling of the hubble-bubble assumed exaggerated proportion.

Unable to bear the suspense, Muratib said: 'If I were you, Maqbool, I should make myself scarce.'

'But you are not me,' Maqbool said with a trace of arrogance in his voice which he tried to convert into humility. 'I am under orders... Besides, I feel that on principle we must struggle... If we believe in freedom from these "Muslim Brethren" as we believed in freedom from the British and their friends...'

He felt priggish after he had said this, especially as he fancied he saw an embarrassed smile on the mouth of Muratib Ali. So he hung his head down in order to beckon that feeling of humility to come to him through which his attitude could become clear to his friend, without explanation, and through which he could summon the necessary strength to move him.

'Principles!' Muratib minced the words between his front teeth. 'Where are the arms to back the principles?'

Maqbool realised that if there had been the armed strength to give the invaders a fight, Muratib might have appreciated the principles.

'The Indian army...' he said, in a voice which betrayed a degree of wishfulfilment.

Muratib merely waved his head, pushed the hookah aside, flushed red and then said: 'Your friends accepted the partition of India! They betrayed their principles! Where is their secular State now?... And they allowed those who believed in divide and rule to dominate the country!... Now, it may be too late even if they do come to our help —'

'But our co-religionists in Pakistan have sold out completely,' said Maqbool with suppressed anger in his voice. 'And you know it!... Do you think these Pakistanis would have come here without the knowledge of the British Commander-in-Chief of the Pakistan army?'

'Too bad,' said Muratib in a doleful tone. 'You have probably heard that they looted my factory...' And he rubbed his hands on the warm Kashmiri dressing gown he was wearing.

Maqbool was sorry for Muratib, though the whining accent of his friend irritated him. For he guessed that Muratib had enough money left over in his Srinagar Bank, as well as in Amritsar and Delhi, where he exported his carpets and shawls, never really to be in need.

'I met Juma and his brothers,' he said to transfer his sympathy to those who deserved it more. 'Their mother does not seem to be frightened to the killers. She was abusing them roundly as I passed by their house. The old woman has spirit...'

'There you go — with your half baked ideas,' said Muratib resentful of Maqbool's lack of sympathy for him and because he could immediately sense an indirect comment on his weakness in Maqbool's praise for Juma's mother.

Maqbool did not say anything, but he felt calm because Muratib's lack of will confirmed his own line of action. At least that much was certain — his love for others, whatever else he knew or did not know. Meanwhile Muratib could live in his separate tragic cycle of cynicism. Surprisingly enough the factory owner's awe-inspiring fatalism was combined with an acute sense of factuality, from the stark statements he had made about politics.

He looked up at the thick set, well-fed frame of his friend, with shy brown eyes and curly hair.

'My mother and wife have been weeping since yesterday,' Muratib said furtively turning his eyes away from Maqbool. 'And I owe a responsibility to them, brother, which I must put before everything else —'

Maqbool realised from these words, what Mahmdoo had taught him by now to sense, that Muratib was deeply involved in his vicious circles.

'I too have a mother, a sister, and a father,' he answered. But again, after he had said these words, he regretted that he had been so gauche and childish, putting his own ego, moth-eaten by fears, against his friend's separateness.

'And I don't suppose you have seen them!' taunted Muratib. 'You went away without telling them where you were going, and they have been hysterical with worry, thinking you were dead or something!'

For a moment, Maqbool felt ashamed to acknowledge the truth of this charge. But he had told his sister where he was going and therein lay his confidence. Muratib was exaggerating. At least Noor could not have been hysterical. She was a good girl and believed in him. She might not have told his mother and father where he had gone, but surely she had reassured them that he was not dead... And they should have understood. For often he had gone out for days into the villages on political work, and, by now, they had surely begun to accept the fact that he was a dedicated person. Somehow, he felt he could not work up that kind of emotion about his family which Muratib felt. And, for good or ill, that was so.

'I told Noor that I was going to Srinagar,' he said tamely. Then after a pause he said, 'One has to do certain things in which one cannot take one's blood relations with one...'

'*Acha*, Hatto, you are a hero!' said Muratib impatiently.

The undercurrent of mockery in Muratib's voice annoyed Maqbool. But he accepted it, and the accompanying hostility, as the well deserved punishment for daring to ask suddenly from a man, whose soul was in pawn to money and privilege and family ties, to abandon all this for what seemed just now to be no more than a slogan or a shibboleth. He sat there, with head hung down.

'To tell you the truth,' continued Muratib, but did not finish.

Maqbool understood from Muratib's face that his presence was not welcome.

'I will go,' he said getting up from the chair abruptly.

But now Muratib jumped up shouting 'no' and went and embraced him and said, with tears in his eyes: 'Maqbool, forgive me, I am a coward! I really do not want you to go...'

'There is no talk,' consoled Maqbool. And with that detached warmth with which the ceremonial embrace between men is conducted, he pressed his torso against Muratib's chest. The passion which he could not work up in himself for his friend had yielded to personal affection.

And now those springs of tenderness were also released in Muratib, which had so far remained hidden in him:

'I know there will be no peace in our land until we have fought them, Maqbool!' the factory owner said, 'I feel sad in my heart... But we are deserted. Everyone seems to have been cowed down. And I have become a coward!...'

'No, no, brother,' interrupted Maqbool separating from his friend. 'We are all liable to fear. Only, if we allow fear to grip our souls, we become cowardly. And each one of us is capable of this, in a situation like the one we are in...'

'Perhaps it is so, but I am not a poet and do not know all the things,' said Muratib sitting down on the edge of his chair, his face covered with his hands. 'But the coterie of friends, that we were, are now separated... You will not accept... I am frightened... And Ghulam is under the thumb of his father. And the only person who could have advised him, your clever friend, lawyer Ahmed Shah, in whom you believed, even against my advice, has gone over...' Saying this he passed his right hand over his forehead and face, as though to cast off the oppression from his visage.

'I was a fool about Ahmed Shah,' agreed Maqbool realising that he had, indeed, been always too impressed by Ahmed Shah's brilliant talk to apprehend his real temperament.

'I remember well,' said Muratib 'that when you made him President of the National Conference branch of Baramula, I told you that he was an opportunist, who would use the movement only for his own ends. He needed that prestige to work up his practice...'

'He had a fairly good practice before,' Maqbool put in as a corrective. But he realised that he himself had never been wise and tended to take people at their word rather than as human beings pulled by different desires and ambitions. 'Though I confess,' he added, 'that you did warn me and you have been proved right... I was not shrewd enough to anticipate his reactions to the changed situation... But Ghulam is, I know, a good man at heart, however he may be swayed...'

'He is weak,' said Muratib. 'Even weaker than me. He cannot cut the connection with his father, as I cannot deny my mother and my wife anything!...'

'I will try to talk to Ghulam,' said Maqbool.

Muratib laughed a little and shrugged his shoulders. And Maqbool became aware that the vague sense of hostility, fear and indifference towards him and the things he represented, was creeping back into his friend's soul. Most people here would feel that, he was sure now. And he thought, nostalgically, of the fighting spirit built up by the friends in Srinagar, the enthusiasm and the doggedness which he had never seen among the people of Kashmir before. How was he to communicate that to his brethren in the occupied town of Baramula?

'Talk is cheap, brother,' said Muratib. 'But what plan have you brought with you? What are we to do?'

'I know you have always despised words,' Maqbool protested. 'I have only a voice. And it is all we can do to talk to each other, to strengthen our morale, to resist in our minds the idea of occupation by the "Muslim brethren". To sabotage their plans and to survive until help comes from Srinagar...'

Muratib looked up at Maqbool and, after all, allowed some real warmth to come into him for the earnestness of his friend. He was even stirred by a wave of admiration.

'If a little money can help,' he said, 'you can have it, frustrate their plans and try to survive until help comes from the drawer.'

Maqbool sensed the measure of Muratib's support and accepted the fact without even a mental protest. Perhaps it was good enough that, inspite of the loss of his factory, Muratib was still offering money. That material support was not to be despised. And though there were too many gaps in Muratib's understanding of the struggle and his sympathies, it seemed that he would, nevertheless, not go against what he, Maqbool, knew was worth struggling for.

'May I go to Ghulam's house?' Maqbool asked Muratib.

'It is dangerous,' said Muratib. 'Go home to your people. I will try and send a message to Ghulam to come and see you...'

'Then he would be in danger,' said Maqbool.

'Here is some money,' Muratib said handing him a wad of notes. Maqbool thrust the notes into his pocket and shook hands with Muratib a little shyly, and, without looking at him, walked away.

'God be with you!' said Muratib contemplating the youthful figure of the poet disappearing into the darkness of the hall on the top of the stairs.

~

Maqbool had to affect the casual effrontery of an inmate of the big house as he came into the lane, freewheeling the bicycle, so that he could will himself into the necessary pose of ordinary behaviour before he should pass by the Pakistani sentry on his way to the house of Ghulam Jilani in the middle of the main bazaar.

This made him feel as though he was striking a semi heroic pose and he relaxed from the dramatic attitude as he actually emerged into the bazaar.

The street was empty, except for a Pathan sentry and some raiders who were sitting on a bench outside the shop of the confectioner, Amira, drinking their morning tea.

The sentry turned to him, as though from habit, even as he held the steaming cup away from his mouth. And, for one instant Maqbool's heart congealed, bringing an involuntary tremor of weakness in his legs. Then, with an almost physical exertion of his will, he converted his dazed apprehension into a smile and, with a loud bluff in his voice, called to the confectioner: 'Amira, Hatto, a cup of hot tea.'

'Come, come, Maqbool Sahib!' the confectioner greeted him. 'Will you have a *kulcha* with your tea?'

'No, you know that I don't eat first thing in the morning,' he said to establish the fact that he was a daily visitor at this shop and he hoped that the name 'Maqbool' by which Amira had addressed him, meant nothing to the Pakistanis.

Amira looked at him a little quizzically, as he began to pour the tea, while Maqbool came and stood, with the saddle of the bicycle resting on his posterior, astride the bench on which the Pathans sat.

'Salt tea or sugar?' asked Amira.

Maqbool winced because such a question was sure to betray him: if he was a regular visitor here, surely Amira would know about his taste. Fortunately, Amira had asked him this in Kashmiri.

'All Kashmiris drink salt tea,' said Maqbool quickly in Punjabi to show that they were not saying anything unusual to each other in Kashmiri. 'I did not know you even made tea with sugar.'

Amira realised that he had been foolish and tried to put the situation back to normal by saying: 'Our guests here prefer tea with sugar.'

'I cannot understand you Kashmiris drinking tea with salt!' commented the sentry in his broken accented frontier Punjabi.

'Foolish folk!' said one of the other Pathans, shaking his head with a trace of arrogance and contempt in his voice.

'They are Muslims, though,' the sentry said, 'like us. Only they have been too long with the infidels!...'

'That Hindu Maharaja is known to be very fond of White women!...' another raider put in. And he winked at his companions.

At this they all laughed and sniggered.

Maqbool too smiled, but tried to cover up his lack of enthusiasm for their talk by taking the cup of tea offered to him by the confectioner.

As he stood back, the handle of the bicycle erratically swerved and he nearly dropped the tea in his confusion.

'Put the steel horse away and sit down here,' the sentry said.

Maqbool took the advice as the easiest way out of the awkward situation.

The tea was scalding hot and he began to blow at it in the spitting-spattering manner of the Kashmiris. And he took advantage of the inclination of his head over the cup to survey the faces of the enemies with surreptitious glances. They were highly tanned, all of them, except for one who was fair-complexioned and blue eyed, with red cheeks. Their torsos bristled with cartridge belts. But their clothes exuded the odour of sour sweat, which came in waves towards his nostrils.

They too became aware of the fact that he was a literate man and somebody. So the sentry asked him as politely as he could in his accented Punjabi. 'Why are the Kashmiris so effeminate!... You ride a woman's steel horse?... Why?...'

'I have a motorcycle,' replied Maqbool knowing that his status would go up immediately if he said this. 'But there is no petrol available... So I borrowed my sister's bicycle.'

Amira was nearly going to rebut this lie with his raised eyebrows but checked himself in time.

Maqbool hurried with his tea, thinking that the longer he stayed here the more difficult conversation might become for him.

'In this they are like us — they drink scalding hot tea!' said the red-cheeked Pathan.

'Also, they eat *naan* and *kulcha*!' said another.

'But they stink!' said another. 'I cannot go near the latrine in the house where I am!... *Toba*! *Toba*!'

'To be sure! To be sure! To be sure!' the others chimed in and laughed.

'*La hol billa*! — talking of the refuse early in the morning!' said the sentry deprecating the unholy talk.

Maqbool had been keeping up a smile as he drank the tea. When he finished with some alacrity, and paid Amira, he directed a *Salam alaikum*, with a hearty bluff, towards the raiders. And then, with a smart sweep of his salwar, he rode off.

'One of our leaders!' blurted out the unfortunate dunce Amira.

Maqbool did not slow down to hear any more, but paddled along the length of a furlong to Ghulam Jilani's house. The stray sentries at the head of other lanes saw him pass. But they had also seen him sitting by their compatriots on the bench outside the confectioner's shop.

When he had gone half way, however, the raiders outside Amira's shop were shouting to the other sentries.

He paddled faster.

But soon a shot rang out beside him.

He did not turn to look, but raced along, aware that they had got to know of him. His legs were collapsing under him, as their shouts tingled in his brain. But his eyes were set almost as though in a reverie. The bitter taste of defeat was in his mouth. He could see Ghulam Jilani's house like a mirage before his eyes. He swallowed the saliva in his mouth, puffed and darted into the gulley, where the side approach to the house lay. He was in luck. The door was open. And Ibil, the old bearded servant, sat smoking the hookah on a charpoy.

'Maqbool!' the old man greeted him warmly for he had known him as Ghulam's friend since they were children.

'Not a word!' Maqbool cautioned him.

And, lifting the bicycle under his arms, he proceeded upstairs, leaving Ibil gasping for breath at the realisation of the danger in which Maqbool might be, considering that he was a firebrand.

~

Ghulam Jilani was pouring tea for a tall handsome stranger and for lawyer Ahmed Shah, as Maqbool entered the big old Kashmir style reception room covered with carpets and cow-tailed cushions. None of the three people on the *diwan* got up as he entered, but all of them looked at him, Ghulam embarrassed and surprised, Ahmed Shah with a contemptuous twist of his mouth, and the stranger with a blank, straightforward stare.

'Come, come,' said Ghulam with an effort at cordiality, 'come and have some breakfast...'

He deliberately avoided welcoming him by name. And Maqbool understood that his friend was seeking to shield him from the stranger, who was presumably one of the officials of the invading army.

'Khurshid Sahib,' began Ahmed Shah in a slightly bantering tone. 'This is Mohammad Maqbool Sherwani!...'

The stranger moved his head briefly, but remained immobile with a conceited smirk on his lips.

Maqbool sensed that Khurshid Anwar knew him to be one of the men of the Kashmir National Movement.

There was no retreat from this situation, because to go downstairs into the street was to court death at the hands of the tribesmen, who had got to know his identity from the confectioner; while, if this man was, indeed, Khurshid Anwar, he, Maqbool, had walked straight into the lion's mouth. However, he rested the cycle by the entrance and walked politely up to sit by the edge of the white table cloth on which breakfast was laid out.

Ghulam Jilani kept his face bent, probably because he did not want to betray any emotion, but his fair complexioned, round visage flushed a vivid red and betrayed his confusion. And he went on pouring the tea in order to keep his eyes averted from all the guests. After he had filled the cup, he put in the milk and two spoons of sugar, and he offered the tea to Maqbool.

Maqbool took it and, affecting a naturalness which he did not feel, said: 'I am sorry to disturb you so early in the morning — without a warning!...'

'When have you ever announced your arrival?' said Ahmed Shah challengingly. 'You workers of the National Conference are like the Communists — always very earnest and very busy.'

Maqbool's first impulse was to return the compliment by reminding him that he himself had once been a President of the Baramula branch of the National Conference; that, in fact, he had manouvered to be elected to this position, but he felt that would be completely unworthy of him. So he kept silent.

Ghulam Jilani's face was like a beetroot now.

For a moment there was a secret exertion of wills and a blind war of impulses in all the four men. The grease congealed on the fried eggs in the plates before the stranger and his cup of tea remained full; while Ahmed Shah ate chunks of bread and butter, even as he picked up a white fried egg his fork so precariously poised that Ghulam Jilani and Maqbool Sherwani both nervously stared at his hands, praying that he would perform the miracle and catch it up in his mouth without dropping it. He did so and they relaxed.

But Ahmed Shah, who had seen them watch his performance, was unnerved enough at the deep roots of his sense of inferiority, and he broke the silence with a violent attack on Maqbool.

'You are a strange person! Never letting us know where you go!... Why were you not here to welcome our friends? You know if you were not our friend, they would never have forgiven your defection to the camp of the Hindu Maharaja... I suppose you have come back now that you know the people of Srinagar are on our side and are ready to welcome — '

'There is no question of forgiveness, as there has been no defection,' Maqbool cut in. 'And the people of Srinagar are not ready to welcome the raiders...'

'They shall soon decide whom they will welcome,' said Khurshid Anwar, provoked by what he considered to be Maqbool's effrontery. 'Our army has outflanked Srinagar, from Gandarbal, and we shall soon make a frontal attack!...'

The strong Punjabi accent of his Hindustani speech annoyed Maqbool on aesthetic grounds, even as Khurshid Anwar's whole

Western Style aggressive personality roused a blind yearning in him to go away from the man's presence. Anwar's English clothes seemed to revive the humiliation at the hands of the White Sahib tourists in Kashmir... But he brought all the self-control he possibly could to bear on his being, though he could not help answering back.

'Why, then, haven't you made the frontal attack?... Are you frightened of the Indian army coming to our rescue?...'

'Oh no!... no, no!' Khurshid Anwar said with a blustering half laugh. 'Let my boys secure the base in Baramula and compensate themselves for their trouble in coming all the way from Peshawar and Abbotabad — then we shall move forward. There are still riches hidden in the houses of Kashmiri Pandits, even if they have taken the Panditanis away!...'

At this Ghulam Jilani blushed visibly. And even Ahmed Shah was ashamed enough to want to cover up the obscene strategy with brave talk.

'Khurshid Sahib is joking, to be sure,' he began. 'But this expedition has been planned by one of the bravest officers of the Pakistan army!... Mr. Jinnah himself is in Lahore, waiting for the good news of our accession to Pakistan. And in Mirpur and Poonch, the Azad Kashmir movement has already set up its own government under Sardar Muhammad Ibrahim... Gilgit has also fallen... Now if only we had sense, we would have voluntarily offered to unite with Pakistan rather than hitch our wagon to the Maharaja's fading star — and Hindu India...'

'There is nothing but contempt in our minds for Maharaja Hari Singh—who has fled with his bag and baggage to Jammu— '

'Cowards can't stand and fight,' Khurshid Anwar said boredly.

'Drink up your tea, Khurshid Sahib,' said the weak Ghulam Jilani, thinking that the only way out of this discussion was to concentrate on breakfast and hope for a miraculous termination of the controversy.

'Don't be so solemn always!' said Ahmed Shah trying to humour Maqbool in case he should flare up against Khurshid Anwar's mockery.

But Maqbool had recognised himself in his own action and was now bent on courting disaster since it had come to him.

'How can you sit by, and see your home town sacked — and looted!... What have we come to?...'

'Why, whose house has been looted?' Ahmed Shah asked. 'Yours?... Have you been home and seen?... Not mine, nor Jilani Sahib's!...'

'Our friend, Muratib has lost his factory,' said Maqbool.

'Only because he was a fool and too mean to give some presents of carpets to our guests!'

'Strange talk!' Maqbool said raising his voice. 'Even friendship seems to mean nothing to you!'

'Don't bark!' challenged Ahmed Shah getting up and pathetically seeking to dominate Maqbool with his small five foot frame.

Ghulam Jilani jumped up and dragged him down with the words: 'Ahmed Shah — Maqbool Sahib differs from you! That is all! Try and convert him! You are a lawyer!...'

'In order to destroy anarchy,' thundered Ahmed Shah, pale in the face, 'we will also resort to anarchy and violence. I believe in reasoning with intelligent men, not with fools!... I want union with Pakistan... I believe in a Central Muslim State, which will be a counter to Communism in the north, and to the Bania Hindu

Raj in the south... And we can connect up with our brethren in the Middle East and revive the glory of ancient Islamic democracy in a world ridden with unbelief!... The poet Iqbal himself preached this. How should this village idiot, pretending to be a poet, know the intricacies of our design, the concept of Muslim federation!... I know more about this than all of you!...'

The last words were so gauche that both Ghulam Jilani and Khurshid Anwar turned their faces away from him.

'You do not believe in your own words,' Maqbool thrust the rapier home. 'How can anyone believe in your words?...'

'I shall murder you!' Ahmed Shah raged and got up again.

This time it was not Ghulam Jilani but Khurshid Anwar who pulled him back: and the latter did not have to use his obvious physical strength, but only a few words: 'You leave that to me, Ahmed Shah!... Just sit down and don't be so jumpy. Let me settle with our friend...'

Ahmed Shah sat down docilely enough.

'Ahmed Shah Abdali's logic!' mocked Maqbool comparing him to the infamous Afghan invader of a century ago.

'Stop mocking at him!' bullied Khurshid Anwar. 'You are not much of a hero either! Running away from home, then sneaking back to spy and curry favour with your rich friends — '

'I have poor friends also,' cut in Maqbool, though he realised the folly of having come here. 'The people will not easily reconcile themselves to this goondaism — '

'Stop this *tain tain* and listen to me,' shouted Khushid with a vulgar tone in his voice, 'I am a straightforward Punjabi and not given to argument... and don't sell me any of your bluff about the people. Islam is a brotherhood in which there are no distinctions, such as the Hindus make — '

'All one happy family in Pakistan!' interrupted Maqbool. 'Mr. Jinnah and the refuges and all! — '

'I have asked you not to interrupt me,' shouted Khurshid Anwar.

'You are not God!' challenged Maqbool, desperate, like an animal at bay and boiling with a violent inner fury.

'No, but listen — I give you a choice: You can have as honourable a place in the brotherhood of Islam as Ghulam Jilani and Ahmed Shah here. Or you will be handed over to our forces to meet the justice due to spies and traitors!'

'I am neither spy nor traitor!... I put Kashmir above everything. I have some principles. And you —'

'It is no use talking to him,' intervened Ahmed Shah. 'A petty, conceited creature. He has not the vision to see anything beyond Baramula. He has never even been to Lahore! And he will not be grateful if you show him mercy. He will want to stab you in the back... A low cur!...'

This abuse cut into the generous spirit of Ghulam Jilani who objected: 'Ahmed Shah Sahib, please do not use such language, Maqbool has been our friend. And as he says, it is a question of his principles. He has chosen his side, as you have chosen yours — '

'Where do you stand, Mr. Jilani?' asked Khurshid Anwar, unnerved, by what seemed like the defection of his host. 'Your father has already decided!'

'To be sure, I am with my father,' said Ghulam Jilani sheepishly. 'But I believe in friendship. I think you can talk to Maqbool and make him see reason. And once he sees it and promises to be with you, he will keep his word — that I can assure you!...'

Having no tact, Khurshid Anwar was persuaded by the superior tact of the landlord's son, seasoned in the courtesies of the court. He knew that the approach suggested by Ghulam Jilani would have been better than the argumentation of Ahmed Shah. He himself had tried to keep calm, but the impetuosity of the lawyer had thrust him into the debate.

'You know your friend better,' conceded Khurshid. 'But you realise that we are living in a time of decision. We cannot just leave things vague. We have to choose!'

'Maqbool is my guest, as you are,' Ghulam Jilani urged, 'And I would not like to misuse the fact of his visit here to impose a decision on him. Nor to ask him to choose immediately. He need not commit himself. He can think things over and see reason — '

'I could only see reason in a reasonable world,' Maqbool said. 'But after this sudden invasion and the murders — '

'This is a war of liberation!' protested Ahmed Shah. 'A war! An historic event! We are passing through times which will decide our destiny forever. And everyone has to choose now!...'

'I will certainly not be bullied up by you,' interrupted Maqbool. 'I don't believe in this historic event — we were living peacefully enough and struggling against wrongs... And then these people came, with guns pointed at us, demanding accession by force — '

'I shall have you arrested, if you don't hold your tongue!' shouted Khurshid Anwar.

The ring of truth in Maqbool's voice seemed to threaten the outer edge of Khurshid Anwar's complacency. So he reacted before his words could penetrate any further into the areas of doubt. For he had his own reasons for being in on this affray, and these were only thinly garbed in the veneer of patriotism.

'Khurshid Sahib, you cannot do anything to my guest,' protested Jilani, beckoning courage from his fat body and reddening in the attempt to do so.

'Ghulam Jilani,' Khurshid answered disclosing the crudeness of his bandit's soul. 'I was going to let you off with the payment of only one lakh as conscience money. It may now become two lakhs —'

'I don't mind the money,' said Ghulam Jilani, 'But you will allow Maqbool to leave.'

'What are you doing and saying?...' protested Ahmed Shah turning to Ghulam Jilani. 'Don't you see?...'

'I am saying or doing nothing which is not according to the traditions of Islam,' said Jilani. 'A guest is sacred to me...'

Maqbool touched Ghulam Jilani's arm tenderly. At this Ghulam got up, with a strange dignity in his roly-poly frame, shook his friend's hand and took him into his arms.

Khurshid looked at this phenomena and was strangely moved.

Maqbool dislocated himself from Ghulam's embrace, and, without heeding Ahmed Shah, walked away towards the door.

'May God be with you!' he mumbled and began to go down the stairs.

'Your cycle,' called Ghulam Jilani.

'It is too dangerous to ride it,' said Maqbool. 'I shall leave it with Ibil downstairs. Send it to the convent to my aunt Rahti. I will have to go through the by-lanes and not on the highway...' And he added bitterly: 'I shall leave the main roads for Ahmed Shah when he goes on the victory parade...'

~

As Maqbool descended the stairs, old Ibil greeted him with a solemn face, which was made more profound by the fingers that he had put on his lips, indicating not a whisper. And he led the young man towards the inner hallway leading to the zenana.

'The Pakistanis are outside, asking for you,' Ibil said.

Maqbool felt very foolish standing there like that with the bicycle under his right arm. Ibil had realised his predicament and, with the tact of the useful uncle, he took the machine from him and put it in the alcove where the fuel wood was stored. Then he came and stood towering over Maqbool and said with a dry wit peculiar to him: 'It is better for a man to ride the machine than for a machine to ride the man.'

Maqbool sensed that old Ibil, having lived through same experiences as everyone else in Baramula, had dropped the opiate insouciance of the servant of the feudal household and seemed to cherish the same simple desire for action and the same anxieties. He was not surprised, therefore, when the man suggested:

'We have to evolve a stratagem by which we can contrive to get you out of this place to some safe hideout... And it has occurred to me that the only way to get you out of here is to lend you the Begum's burqah, also a female attendant. Then the Pathans will not dare to look your way... They still have some respect for the wife of the landlord...'

Before such logic Maqbool could only bow respectfully, though he tried to make sure.

'But the Begum Sahib — '

'I have already told the Begum Sahib you are upstairs. And she has expressed the wish to see you. So you come with me. I shall get my wife, Habiba, to escort you by way of the sub-lane to the main bazaar to your house.'

Maqbool watched the old man's wizened face and saw the warmth which transfused it. As he looked steadily, tears came into his own eyes. And, before they became obvious, he began to walk towards the zenana as Ibil followed.

'The Begum Sahib may be in her bath,' said Ibil coming forward. 'I shall go ahead of you.' And immediately, he called out: 'Habiba — Maqbool Sahib is here, Will the Begum Sahib...?'

There was a fluttering of forms and confused whispers, so that both Maqbool and Ibil halted deliberately to wait and give the females time for cover. At length Habiba answered: 'Come in. I am just putting henna on Begum Sahiba's head!'

Maqbool stepped forward, with his head bent. But he was able to take in the situation. Begum Mehtab Jilani was seated on her diwan, while Habiba was plastering the red dye on her hair.

'Maqbool, son, there is no purdah from you,' the Begum said. 'But what a time you have chosen to arrive!'

'I am unlucky,' Maqbool said realising that, apart from her hospitality, she too, like her son, wished he had not embarrassed her household with his awkward presence.

'Come and sit down by me,' the Begum said.

Maqbool obeyed as docilely as he had always done as a child.

'Habiba,' Ibil beckoned to his wife.

The maid looked at the Begum and the mistress nodded her head.

'Life is cruel,' the Begum began philosophically. 'As a woman I have known this truth. We have to accept, because in the eyes of Allah, we deserve the punishment. The only way, son, in which this cruelty can be offset is by obedience to destiny. What is written in one's fate will be... I was born a woman. So it was no use my protesting against fate. I had to accept, but acceptance brought contentment. I must admit that, when I came, as a young woman, to the house of Sardar Jilani, I was afraid. I decided to obey him. I could not do certain things, and yet everything was really in my hands. He ruled me, but I ruled the household... Now these new rulers demand obedience. But, perhaps, if we accept their rule, we will be free to do what we like in our own households... Only Allah, the just, knows everything...'

'If I may say so, respectfully,' said Maqbool, 'when death is opposed to life then life must oppose death... I know there will be much bloodshed, and ruin in this way, but the urge for freedom cannot be suppressed...'

'I know that you are as determined as all the young are,' Begum Mehtab conceded. 'And I always pointed you to my son as an example of sacrifice. But you will understand that my husband and I, and our son, have bigger responsibilities than most people.'

'I know — ,' said Maqbool bitterly.

'Son,' she said briefly. 'We have to take refuge in our love for our family — and in our belief in God...'

There was silence between them.

'I know you opinion, son,' the Begum continued. 'But we have treated all our tenants as our children. Only, they are people who cannot rule themselves. They need a gentle, wise father. And Sardar Sahib has always been that at heart, however harsh he may have seemed at times — '

The words jarred on Maqbool's ears, because in his consciousness, poverty, and even the abject acceptance of that poverty by the peasantry, had become the root of all evil in Kashmir. All the hierarchy of the feudal order, from the Maharaja downwards, through his courtiers and landlords, represented a chain of humiliations which had only to be seen and lived through to be believed, of course, in the sequestered shades of the zenana of the landlord's house, the whole array seemed a permanent god-given order which had to be accepted and obeyed.

'Mother,' he said with a trace of impatience in his voice. 'We can never decide this argument. Some day perhaps you will realise that I didn't lead your son astray as you always thought I did... But he and I have been like brothers. And, even now, at the risk of the displeasure of Khurshid Anwar, he has protected me from the invaders. You have always been to me like a mother... I want to go from your presence, as a good son and not a quarrelsome *shaitan* boy...'

Begum Mehtab put her left hand on his head and said: 'But you better stay here now. Where can you go at this time, with them on all sides?'

'Begum Sahiba,' said Ibil coming forward. 'I have a plan if you will permit it. Maqbool Sahib will go in your burqah and Habiba will go with him, from the door in the small lane where there are no enemies...'

'Ibil!' said the Begum imperiously. 'Do not call them enemies. It is not seemly. But perhaps Maqbool's only way home is the way you suggest... You better ask Abdul, to yoke the horse to the tonga, and escort them yourself... To be sure, this is the best — '

She did not finish her sentence. But her heavy jaw fell with the painful pull between her humanity and the instinct for the preservation of her family.

Maqbool bowed very low to her as he rose and followed Ibil.

'I will go into the inner room,' the Begum said to enable them to carry out the arrangement without being actually involved in them. 'Habiba, come back quickly. I shall be anxious about you...' And she went into the inner sanctums of the zenana.

~

Seated beside Habiba, huddled like a ghost in the burqah with the *jallied* aperture, before his eyes in the hood of the veil, disclosing nothing but the blue curtain at the back of the tonga to guard female decorum against the intrusion of strangers' stares. Maqbool went through the queerest experience of all his life. That he, Maqbool Sherwani, should go in a woman's veil seemed humiliating and foolishly histrionic. And yet it was an old strategem of the feudal households. But wouldn't the Pakistanis be reckless enough to look in to make sure...

The carriage had jog-trotted quite fifty yards without anything happening.

Perhaps, he felt, that the sentries outside the house of Sardar Muhammad Jilani had seen the tonga issue from the exalted one's residence and given the password to the other sentries. Still Ibil was playing with his own life, and that of his wife's in escorting him. For, if the raiders had suspected that he, Maqbool Sherwani, had probably gone into the Jilani household (since they had come knocking on the door), then the very sight of the landlord's servant would make them suspicious.

The rhythmic jolting of the horse carriage unnerved him, and he sweated inside the veil and quivered. The uneven ruts in the road shook him. And he found his mind emptying into the vacancy of suspense.

'Who is there?' suddenly a Pathan sentry challenged.

'From the household of Sardar Jilani,' answered Ibil.

Soon there was the clattering of hobnailed shoes and muffled voices.

The impulse to live hovered on the fearful threat of being found out. But Maqbool looked before him without stirring. Suddenly, the purdah at the back of the tonga was lifted by two soldiers.

'Who?' one of the Pathans barked.

'Zenana,' said Habiba.

For a while, the soldiers who had not spoken, lingered and stared hard at the forms.

'Why do you annoy even females?' Ibil said aggressively. 'Among Muslims this is not done.'

The soldier dropped the curtain.

'Go ahead,' Ibil said to the coachman.

Maqbool had held his breath. The grip of his mouth was tight in spite of him and his eyes had closed. The miracle had happened again. Rescued from the very jaws of death! Would his luck hold out? he wondered. Instinctively, he found himself with the word Allah at the back of his head in thankfulness... And he reflected how strange it was that those who were, on principle, the life oposers, the family of the landlord, should have saved him at the risk of courting the displeasure of their newfound friends.

The carriage advanced slowly. But in order to keep the occupants at the back informed of where they were, Ibil went on directing the coachman: 'There' he said, 'stop by the shop of the confectioner. ...And wait here till I return!...'

And, in a moment, the tonga came to a standstill.

'Please alight and I will escort you,' Ibil announced to the occupants.

Maqbool allowed Habiba to get down first. Then he got down. Ibil came near him and whispered: 'The road is clear.'

And he led the way into the gulley.

~

Awkward and halting, in spite of his best efforts, Maqbool advanced with an affected slouching gait behind Ibil, his heart beating involuntarily.

As they got to the middle of the lane, Ibil said in an almost audible speech:

'The sentries of this lane have taken the confectioner with them to identify someone they suspect...'

Habiba shushed him from behind the lifted headpiece of her burqah. And she led the train up to the door of Maqbool's house. And she even took the initiative in striking the suspended latch of the door to summon the household from above. Fortunately, out of the fear of the raiders, the lane was empty, except for prying eyes, who only saw the females of Sardar Jilani's house enter with the servant, Ibil, when the door was opened by Maqbool's mother.

Habiba went to Maqbool's mother and turning her eyes to the other form in burqah, whispered: 'Maqbool.'

Maqbool's mother was dazed and stared uncomprehendingly at the figure before her.

Maqbool seemed to have surveyed the hall through the eyepiece of the burqah, and, finding the place empty, he took off the veil.

His mother put her arms around him and clung to him weeping.

'Mother, mother,' he called to her to silence her.

'I thought you were dead, Maqbool...' she sobbed. 'I thought they had killed you!'

At that instant, Maqbool's father came down, a lean, pale man with a grim and angry expression on his face.

Maqbool greeted him respectfully, almost as a stranger accosts an official: '*Salam alaikum!*'

The old man answered equally formally: '*Wa alaykum as-salam!*'

'Where is Noor?' Maqbool asked.

'She is upstairs, son,' his mother said. 'So are other people — all waiting for you. Mahmdoo of the cookshop from Pattan is here. And his son, Gula. And others... We were all worried about you. Come... And you must be hungry...'

And she led the way upstairs.

'When Gula went there at dawn to fetch you,' said Mahmdoo, the fat confectioner, 'and did not find you there, I thought that either the worst had happened and they had caught you, or that you had come home... So I asked the way here... I am happy you have come back safe. ...These *shaitans* are everywhere...'

'But too busy looting to be very vigilant,' Maqbool put in. 'Even their leader, Khurshid Anwar, is sitting comfortably at Sardar Jilani's house to take his tribute from there, before he will do anything else. And he said his men must collect enough to compensate themselves before moving on to Srinagar — '

'One lakh is what he demands,' said Ibil, who, like all servants in a feudal household, seemed to know everything that was going on. 'Sardar Sahib had promised him fifty thousand, which is all he had in cash... The Master had gone to fetch that from the safe in the shop when you came home...'

All those assembled uttered moans of wonder and horror when they heard such big sums being mentioned. Only Maqbool protested: 'I would like to stop him from paying that money to this robber and crook!'

'Son, you use strong words,' Maqbool's father intervened sternly.

'Such robbery with violence calls for strong words, father!' said Maqbool.

'Now, no quarrel in your household,' the mother said. 'The tea is ready. Noor, my child, bring the *samovar* over here and I will pour it.'

Maqbool's sister, Noor, an even featured girl, slightly disfigured by the pimples of youth, which she had squeezed, came over with the samovar and crouched near the company demurely, keeping her bright big eyes lowered even as she drew the headcloth over her forehead.

'You have always encouraged these children to disobedience,' said the father turning to the mother.

'Begum Jilani also believes that the highest thing in life is obedience!' Maqbool said. 'All the old people believe in obedience. We must accept and not rebel. All that happens to us is due to the fate ordained by Allah!... Say five prayers a day, keep the fasts and obey — and die in the process!...'

The tone of mockery in Maqbool's voice disturbed his mother who wanted the happy family reunion to last out in the atmosphere of cordiality. So long as her chickens were safe in her coop, she felt no concern about anything outside.

The father remained silent at the rebuke, which his son had administered to him by implication. Then he burst out from the strange cavern of his fears and frustration.

'What can we do against such odds; I ask you! The salvation of our souls lies in the hands of Allah and his prophets. If we pray, perhaps Allah will hear our prayers...'

'But father,' Noor ventured, 'our brother loves the weak. He has been working for others. How can you expect him to rest content with prayers... Allah does not seem to hear — '

'Silent... Noor, and don't blaspheme!' shouted the father. 'I should not have sent you to that school!...'

'Pour the tea, child,' the mother consoled Noor quickly lest the girl should burst into tears as she usually did at the least little rebuke.

'Allah has sent his apostles, the Pakistanis, our "Muslim brethren", to liberate us by depriving us of our breath!' said Maqbool with a caustic and bitter humour.

'The whole house is in revolt against me!' protested the father.

'To be sure!' Mahmdoo intervened, out of embarrassment at the family quarrel. 'But, all the same, Maqbool Sahib has been known as the friend of broken people! He is a worthy son. And you ought not to feel that he is doing anything wrong if he wants us to struggle against the invaders. Our leaders have sent him to Baramula...'

This silenced the company. And Maqbool's mother used the tense calm to serve tea to everyone. Noor looked at her brother surreptitiously from the corners of her eyes, full of admiration for her brother, who had actually been talking to the great in Srinagar. Gula broke the reserve by saying naively:

'Maqbool, brother, when shall we go to Pattan to collect the motor cycle? Will you take me to Srinagar on it?'

At this Mahmdoo laughed a brief laugh and then turned on his son:

'We are all in danger of our lives — and you, fool, think only of the motor cycle!'

'The trouble with our leaders,' began Maqbool's father, 'is that they are idealists! They love the poor, but do not realise that the poor cannot love them. All the people want is bread. And, for the rest they lie about unheeding on the dung heaps! And they have no thought of Allah...'

'You should be in Srinagar, father,' said Maqbool, 'to see how much those whom you despise work. It is not their fault if they are unheeding. You know how the *Angrezi Sarkar* has ground us down and made life as cheap as dust... Do you think that we do not believe in anything?... But we cannot save the soul of a person without saving his body... We must survive... The trouble is that, in spite of their prayers, they have lost faith — they no longer seek to live by any truth in their lives...'

'You talk some sense, son,' conceded the father looking away from Maqbool and turning to his hookah, which Noor had filled for him. And he continued: 'But then often you become mad and talk like a fanatic!...'

'He is young,' apologised the mother. 'And he has reduced himself to a skeleton rushing about. He neglects to eat or drink — and he has become impatient. I would like to feed him on good food for at least a month when all this is over. Mahmdoo, you must send us some good butter from Pattan. I hear the cowherds come to your shop daily with milk and butter...'

'To be sure, the mother of Maqbool,' assured Mahmdoo. 'I shall send you the good ghee as soon as this blight — '

There was the sound of knocking at the door and the faces of the whole company became pale. For a moment, the suspense hung before their wide open eyes.

Maqbool's mother looked out of the window of the sitting room and quickly turned to reassure everyone: 'Juma and his brothers!...'

'We shall beg your permission to go,' said Ibil. And he turned to Habiba, who had sat huddled up in her burqah by the shoes on the door.

Maqbool got up and saw Ibil to the door, so that he could give him some cash for his trouble. Inside the little hall, beyond the doorway, he put a ten rupee note into Ibil's hand and shook the closed fist warmly with both his own hands...

Noor came up to him as he turned and said: 'Brother, take me with you to Srinagar if you go again. I can ride on the back of your motor cycle.'

Maqbool touched her cheek tenderly and said in a bantering manner:

'Noori, you will first have to get mother to allow you to wear a salwar and kurta rather than this Kashmiri gown before you can become a soldier.'

'Nothing of the kind!' warned the mother who had overheard. 'No girl of mine will become a soldier. I won't trust her out of this home, with those brutes about!...'

'But mother,' assured Maqbool. 'All the young boys and girls in Srinagar have joined the military and are learning to use guns!'

'Father, I also want to go to Srinagar,' said Gula impetuously. 'Send me with Maqbool!'

'And we too want to go there!' shouted Juma. 'To Srinagar —'

'War is no joke,' Maqbool's father answered. 'There are bullets about.'

'Hatto, he has just come from Srinagar,' added Mahmdoo. 'He can't go back there without running into danger!...'

'But we can't sit here, twiddling our thumbs,' said Juma.

'Especially when there is no work,' said Qadri, who was the most gentle of the three brothers.

'And I for one am through with work at the factory,' said Saleem Bux. 'I want to join the army —'

'And see the world!' mocked Mahmdoo.

'It is good to hear this talk,' commented Maqbool. 'At least the young want to do something... Not like all the old ones who want to cave in... In Srinagar even the old have enlisted in the volunteer corps — '

'I suppose even the old people learn to recognise the needful when someone can make the choice for them,' said Mahmdoo. 'We had lost everything. Now there is a cause!...'

'I understand the rich not being able to make a choice,' said Maqbool. 'I have met Muratib Ali and Ghulam Jilani. They were good friends of mine. But they are behaving like weaklings, because they are privileged. For those who are not privileged the choice is easier. We must fight against the violent destroyers of life — with violence. There is such a thing as goodness and honesty — as there is evil and lies! We are not, like the Pakistanis, exhorting people to go and slaughter! We are innocent enough. And we have been attacked. We have to fight against the invasion... Against the tribesmen — ours is the human response of pity for those whom they have despoiled!...'

The fact that he was standing as he said all this gave his words authority, though he deliberately avoided an oratorical tone of speech. For he had a horror of claptrap and mere shouting, being essentially a reserved adolescent, recognising few imperatives except those which flowed from the poet and school-teacher in him.

His father sensed the truth of his words and stole out to the kitchen to help himself to more live coal for his hookah.

The warmth which came from Maqbool's physique drew Noor to him more ardently than she might, at that age, have been drawn to by any lover. Her face glowed as she removed the empty cups from before the guests and poured tea for the newcomers. Then she saw Maqbool's cup lying full of cold tea.

'But,' she said with her own small voiced humour now that father was out of audible distance. 'Your cup is full to overflowing!...'

'Oh, Saki,' Maqbool repeated the hackneyed phrase of poetry. 'Bring me a new hot cup of salt tea...' And he smiled at her, even as he turned to Juma, Qadri and Saleema and Mahmdoo...

They warmed to him and turned to him, expecting to speak.

He looked at them and then began:

'All the way to Srinagar I was obsessed by the thought of writing a poem on the terrors of death. But when I got there I saw so much life, so much of life that my fears fell away from me. It is a question of faith, of belief in ourselves and in the struggle... And then we can hope to be free... I went through all kinds of moods on the road. I lived through the moods of the people. I thought of their resignation before Allah. But something in me could not accept, though I was spiritless enough, until I saw the people of Srinagar... Then the spirit came into me. And all my being rose in protest against the evil which has been thrust upon us... Now we cannot ignore the sincere faith which the people of Srinagar have put into us — the people of Baramula. They expect us to hold out. I know that death is not an amusing thing. And I realise that it may be difficult here. And then, at the end — it won't be like a fairy story, happy ever after. But we will still have to wage a persistent struggle. We will have to suffer, and suffer... But that is how men grow — become men...'

There was a knocking at the door downstairs. This time mother being away, Noor looked out of the window. A whole group of Pathans was there, shouting:

'That bandit Maqbool is up there? Send him down! The son of a donkey! He has given us the slip twice!'

Noor returned from the window, pale and speechless.

'Go and hide,' she said to Maqbool.

By this time his mother and father had gone, running to the windows, while Jumma, Qadri, Saleem Bux, and Mahmdoo, got up to take cover.

'Maqbool is not here,' his father lied.

'Open the door!'

'Go away,' Maqbool's mother shrieked.

And she was answered back with profanities.

Mahmdoo came forward and, detaching the fainting Noor from Maqbool, thrust the boy away, saying: 'Run, if you can... go ... somewhere...'

The shrewd glance in Mahmdoo's eyes contrasted with the vulnerable tenderness in his voice: 'Go, go...'

'Go away and hide,' whispered Juma.

Maqbool passed his hand over Noor's forehead and looked around desperately. Then, with a jerk of his head, he had decided: 'I will go to the haystack,' he said to Mahmdoo.

'I am coming with you,' said Gula.

'Gula!' Mahmdoo snarled at his son.

But his son had already gone ahead towards the kitchen and waited there to follow Maqbool.

'The only way out is from the rooftop,' Noor said opening her eyes wide. 'Come, I will show you...'

And she got up to go and show her brother, but collapsed on hearing heavy steps behind her. The Pakistanis had broken the door downstairs, and were rushing up when Maqbool mounted the steps to the loft of the house from which the window led to the roof top.

As the sentries came into the sitting room, holding the confectioner, Mahmdoo, before them, they shouted.

'Where is he? Son of the Devil!... Identify him!'

The man waved his hand emptily.

'Rooftop, rooftop!' Noor was moaning in Kashmiri. 'Maqbool hurry away to the rooftop...'

'What does she say?' one of the sentries queried, his red beard glowing like fire.

The confectioner could not speak. But even against his will, his eyes roamed towards the direction where Maqbool had gone.

'The swine, he has given us the slip again. Follow him... up there!... It seems he has gone there...'

Maqbool crouched on the precarious edge of the sloping roof of his father's house to survey the position. It would be best to get on to the flat roofs of the houses at the end of the lane and then jump off from there to the fields.

Before he had decided to do this, however, he heard steps coming up to the loft. So there was no time to pause and think. He must run for it.

A strange stillness was in his soul. Then panic. His heart drummed. And in front of him he could see the hazards of treading on the tin gutter into which the wooden roof ended. Ten yards of it, before he could reach the first flat roof, of the house of the carpenter Akbar. He took the chance.

Crashing of old tin bending under his feet... Crackling of dead leaves... And crunch-crunch of the wooden supports.

The sunlight from the even blue sky guided him in a half playful mood. The odds were that either the tin would give way, and he would fall to his death: or that his pursuers would snipe at him and pick him off, because they were such wonderful marksmen. Or that he would get past the width of his own house into Akbar's roof...

He found himself getting to the first objective...

As he had half expected, a bullet rang through behind him, just missing his left arm.

He must be bearing a charmed life, for the fire had come almost from thirty yards away.

He wriggled, in spite of himself, feeling he had been shot, though he knew he was safe.

This made him turn his face to the small window of the loft, and he saw that the sniper was the sentry to whom he had spoken at the confectioner's shop.

He drucked his head behind the projection of the sloping roof and waited for the next move.

Only foul mouthed abuse. And the challenge: 'Come out!'

A prolonged moment.

Apparently the sentry was trying to decide whether he should follow him or adopt some other strategy.

This gave Maqbool time to measure the distance from Akbar's roof to the house at the end of the lane. About a hundred and fifty yards...

He would have to walk, exposed on roofs and walls. And the next bullet may get him.

He would wait.

'Surround all the houses!' the Pakistanis were shouting. 'And shoot him!'

From the cover which he had taken, it was three yards to the thick wall of Akbar Khan's house. He breathed deeply and tried to get his nerve back.

Instinctively, he lifted the lapel of his shirt to offer a target.

The shot inevitably followed. He had reckoned on five seconds before the sentry could reload.

So he darted towards the wall.

Another bullet coursed down, by him.

There was no escape. He jumped into the sloping roof of the verandah of Akbar Khan's house. Then, without pause, he leapt into the courtyard.

Shrieks... Shouts... Weeping...

But he was set for his objective — the door.

He unlocked the latch and emerged into the lane.

The pursuers had all entered the hall of his own house and the coast was clear.

He ran.

Panting, almost exhausted, his hands grazed badly, he took the curve of the lane, cleanly, almost as a master sprinter. His eyes were nearly blind with the smoke of confusion. His heart beat like the drum of the tribesmen, speaking his death knell with each beat. He moaned involuntarily.

Then a barrage of rifle fire opened up behind him. Bullets whizzed past. Obviously, they had come down from his father's house. Not too near yet. But they might catch up with him.

One cartridge went into the side of a door ahead, into old Rajba's house.

Shouts.

They must be following now.

He leapt over the projection by Zooni's the weaver woman's house.

He skipped over the hens, which went fluttering before him, cackle, cackle...

Silence.

Again shouts, abuse and challenges.

He couldn't tell who was encouraging him to run and who was asking him to stop.

His mother must be weeping, his sister must have fainted... 'Thanks be to Allah!' his father must be saying...

Allah! Where was Allah! Why was he always against the innocents?... There would be no salvation unless the religion of fate went by the board and the soul became alive?... Noor's face was like a crumpled flower before his forehead — as she lay helpless!... And his mother's drawn face, uglied by fear... at the back of his head. But his father's face did not appear! Anyhow, how could God punish them so?...

The strong uprush of feelings made for slowness.

He pulled himself together, looked back and saw his pursuers running in a horde, nearly overpowering him.

That moment of the vision of his enemies became a prolonged agony — so clear was the picture of heads and torsos, with rifles pressing forward.

He put all his will into the race to get away.

Another barrage of fire.

One bullet at his heels.

He jumped.

It would be safer to keep leaping.

Perhaps they didn't want to kill him outright. That was why they were shooting at his feet.

As he jumped and came down on earth, his right foot fell in the large greazy puddle of the open drain and slipped on the slime.

He fell head long.

What a stupid thing to do! The fellows must be right on him.

He heaved himself from where he lay and stood up.

The advance guard of the pursuers was on him.

Hitting him with the rifle ends, shouting abuse and filth in their broken speech, slapping his face, and thrusting their fisticuffs into his sides, they pulled him from side to side, slapped him again and pushed him forward, till he fell.

They dragged him up and, supporting his sinking form, pushed him forward again, the forth of anger in their shouting, crazed mouths.

~

The Pakistanis took him to the courtyard of an old caravanserai, which had been used, until their descent upon the town, as stables-cum-residential quarters by the tongawallahs of Baramula.

The dirty, bare courtyard was congested with a horde of tribesmen, who sat drowsily on string charpais, leaning on their bedrolls and gossiping, as the hookah gurgled in their midst. Most of the ferocious men stared somnolently at the prisoner as he came in, ahead of the rifle points of his captors. Maqbool felt so self-conscious that he did not raise his eyes and went blindly forward.

'A *kafir!*' one of the guards announced to his brethren.

For a moment, the hubble-bubble did not gurgle anymore, as all eyebrows were raised towards the victim. Then some horses, tied to halters at one end of the stables, neighed in succession, as though they were sensitive to Maqbool's plight. And the congeries of men began to pass comments to each other.

Maqbool felt the strong tang of the dung that had been scattered by the horse's hoofs into the courtyard and he noticed huge flies buzzing on the refuse.

As his attention was distracted, a tall, lanky man, with a cartridge belt slung from his left shoulder to the right side of his waist, came over and accosted him.

'Oh, do you not value your life — that you defy us?'

Maqbool felt the impulse to be histrionic and answer back, but he restrained himself.

His captors made what sounded like a report in a staccato speech to the tall fellow, who gave some orders to the guards. As a result of this exchange, his captors pushed him towards the little door of a cell.

'The orders of Zaman Khan,' one of the guards bawled, 'you will remain here till Sardar Khurshid Anwar comes to decide your fate.'

Maqbool felt a tremor of relief at the thought of being out of their reach for a while, if even for a little while. He willingly went forward, feeling the mouths of the rifles still digging into his back. At length Zaman Khan advanced, unlatched the iron latch from the hook on the panel of the rather battered old style door, and flung it open. One of the captives viciously kicked him from behind, so that he nearly fell headlong into the dungeon, but was saved by the end of a huge bedstead which occupied half the room. An instinctive groan escaped him: 'This will make you into a believer, infidel!' said the guard who had kicked him.

Zaman Khan gave further orders even as he closed the door and fastened the latch in its place.

Maqbool's heart pounced fiercely in spite of his will to suffer what was coming, as the inevitable punishment for his rebel's pride.

~

In the darkness of the narrow, cavernous Mughal style cell, apparently the home of a tongawallah from the broken leather straps which hung on the pegs on the wall, Maqbool came face to face with his own fears.

He seated himself on the bed, his legs dangling from the perch.

All kinds of thoughts rushed through him. What would his parents be thinking? To be sure, his mother must be weeping, his father sullen and angry, and his sister sad and shedding tears in secret as was her habit. If only he could have been allowed to talk to them at length, to comfort them and to tell them that he had decided to fight it out and die, he would have been content.

But these barbarians had pushed him out. Strange that their slogan was 'Allah ho Akbar!' As he was not a Muslim at all, but only born a Muslim, he need not be shocked, he felt. He had not said the Friday prayers for a long time — no prayers at all since the last Id day, and that was also because there was the feast of sweet vermicelli to follow the morning's ritual in the mosque. He recalled that his mother had asked him to keep at least one fast as a token during the holy month of Ramzan, but he had always laughed away her pleas and said that, as a political agitator, he kept so many enforced fasts, forgetting to eat while wandering from village to village... So the raiders were, after all, being just, from their point of view. To them, it was 'jehad', a holy war, in which all the defenders, and their friends, were infidels who must be destroyed... There was something terrible about this singlemindedness, which drove people to the extremes of brutality without a stirring of their consciences... because he himself would have had doubts before killing people...

In the gloom of the cell, however, such self righteousness seemed only a way of consoling the heart, as it were.

Apart from the terror that impinged on his consciousness from every side, the low ceiling, made of rough, wooden planks, over which were the heaps of the tongawallah's belongings, all covered with back soot of hearth fires, weighed him down.

He saw a cockroach steadily advancing between the planks and he realised that there must be other insects about in the cell, possibly scorpion and rats, and even a snake. His eyes wandered across the dirty surface of the string bed and he was sure that there would be bugs in it. The instinct for the clean life that had always made him recoil back from the disarray of his own home and the squalor in the huts of the poor he visited, assailed him, and his soul shrank at the realisation that if he had to stay here for the night the insects would certainly creep over his body.

Suddenly, he felt that his own clothes were sodden and grimy and torn, and a kind of nausea arose in his mouth, which was partly aroused by the acrid stink of the atmosphere and partly from the thirst for water which possessed him, as also from self disgust.

As he became aware of his thirst, this feeling began to overpower all the rest. He smacked his tongue to quench the thirst, only to find that the nausea increased with the licking.

His eyes explored the gloom of the cell for the pitcher of water that he imagined must be there. And, now, used to the gloom, he traced the curve of a vessel by the oven. He dashed forward and found a glazed earthen cup covering the pitcher in the corner. Impetuously, bending the pitcher on one side, he filled the cup and drank the water, only discovering as he did so, that the liquid was stale. Then, suddenly, he felt the urge to pass water. This awkward but real thing seemed to be almost the final humiliation. He was confused and embarrassed by it, and began to feel the poignancy of the absurd situation, which was like the awful predicament he had faced as a child in school once when the schoolmaster would not listen to his plea and he had done it in his salwar.

After a moment's hesitation, and a few circular steps in the middle of the room, he became convinced that the only dignity lay in defying his own self-respect, and going to a corner in the dark.

After he had gone through the disgust aroused by the foetid atmosphere, he sat back on the bed, a little calmer, though still with the lingering horror against squalor inside him.

The absence of any significant odour seemed to clear his conscience. And he had the momentary illusion of being born again, though, immediately, he met the fact of frustration, the anxiety which had always seemed to him to be the point in the curve of his life at which his fate always seemed suspended in the air.

He had the apperception that the verdict of Khurshid Anwar would result in his being strung up in the courtyard of the square, his blood would be clotted on the earth amid the dung of the stables, his body drained of life, all looking so horrible that no one would be able to contemplate it. He felt he would accept that, if only to be out of this dark chamber. Only, perhaps his sister Noor would come and see the carcass hanging up there — and tears of self-pity came into his eyes. And he felt he must at least write her a final message.

His eyes now explored for the light. And, instinctively, he went towards the chinks in the door. By riveting his eyes about an inch or two away from the line of light he could perhaps write.

He sat down on the earth, resting his back on the door. The light was so thin, he would have to adjust himself sideways.

He felt for his notebook and pencil in the pocket of his tunic and found it was there. For a while, his mind meandered in the many dimensions of the darkness before him, in the gradations of vague feelings and the confusion of the unknown experiences yet to come. Then he had the feeling of Noor's long plaits of hair, the way he used to pull them to tease her, to be affectionate to her. And with the feel of the plaits, came the memory of her hands, as they lay dropped on the pillow in her sleep, the swift eager movements of her limbs in the kitchen and the virgin's tenderness in her eyes... He began to scribble:

'My little sister, Noor, we shall not see each other.'

The act of writing with the little pencil in the light of the chink in the dark relaxed his spirit and he persisted.

~

Time had been more or less destroyed for him while he wrote to his sister, because he deliberately expected the worst to happen. But during the long wait for something to happen, he tried to imagine that, beyond him, life was going on. And when he knew that this was so, he was full of envy for those who were still active, aching to be there with them, alive...

Then, suddenly, there was a hubbub in the courtyard, and through the chink of the door, he saw Khurshid Anwar arrive at the head of a little procession, with little round Ahmed Shah leading the train.

The tribesmen in the courtyard got up and bowed, taking their hands to their foreheads to the accompaniment of salutations.

'Where is the traitor Sherwani?' asked Ahmed Shah stepping forward.

Tall Zaman Khan pointed to the cell.

'Arrange a charpai for Khurshid Sahib,' Ahmed Shah said. 'We will try the infidel here and now.'

Some of the soldiers who had been seated on a bedstead near the cell, along with Zaman Khan, in the capacity of watchmen, scattered away, thus leaving a little clearing before the charpai.

Ahmed Shah ran a little caper and, spreading a blanket on the bedstead, smoothed it for Khurshid Anwar to sit upon.

Meanwhile, Zaman Khan proceeded towards the cell, and, unlatching the door, faced Maqbool Sherwani, who had been waiting, with his eyes glued to the chinks in the door.

'Come out,' Zaman Khan said surlily. And then he called three soldiers to come and receive him.

Maqbool's heart, the troubled heart, was beating in spite of himself. He anticipated the worst. And though he had seen his judges come into the courtyard, the suspense was terrible.

The three warders dragged him out, then pushing the mouths of their rifles into him, they thrust him forward before Khurshid Anwar's improvised court.

The interrogation began without much formality, with a broadside from Ahmed Shah, who strutted about in his self-appointed role of public prosecutor.

'Why oh, *kafir?* Are you still unrepentant?'

Maqbool was dumb at the effrontery of this man, who seemed so anxious to please his new masters. His mind, deadened by the hours he had spent in the cell, had not yet got used to the light.

He could not comprehend the process by which a person, supposedly human, could suddenly become a turncoat. He vaguely ascribed the change, in Ahmed Shah's attitude, to ambition and greed, and, instinctively, he knew these to be the compensation which the little round man required for his lack of physical height.

He sat down on his haunches, instead of answering his ex-friend's questions.

Ahmed Shah advanced in a fury and kicked him, so Maqbool fell back.

Dazed by the assault, the victim just watched the lawyer, still unable to believe that the thread of connection between the two Kashmiris should break so completely through the change in political allegiances. Somehow, he could not believe in the scene in which he was involved. He had the hallucination of being in hell. And they all seemed like the angels of Gabriel — frightening monsters. For he despised them all, more even than they hated him. And in his heart he was free of them, from the strength of what he believed to be his larger sympathies as against their crude insults. The combination of this belief, and the strange itch of irreverence against the chosen race of the Muslim brotherhood in his limbs, almost made him smile.

But he controlled himself from expressing himself against the force of this trial and sat up, surveying his tormentors from the corners of his reddened eyes, blinking every now and then, as though to adjust himself to the solid reality of Khurshid Anwar and the soldiers before him, and the antics of Ahmed Shah, the solid round pillar of the new society. He felt angry as a lion watching the incomprehensible feats of the tormentors who were twisting his tail, as it were.

At least the oracle spoke through the sharp, clear Punjabi voice of Khurshid Anwar: 'Answer the questions which are going to be put to you. Otherwise we shall have to extort your confession by other means... And, if even now you repent and realise that you were born a Muslim, and not a Kafir, we will forgive you... Zaman Khan, stand there by him — and — '

Ahmed Shah cut into Khurshid Anwar's utterance: 'Sardar Khurshid Anwar is being generous to you in the hour of our victory. Tonight our army will be in Srinagar. So I give you the chance to recant. Repeat after me: "I give up my membership of the Kashmir National Conference..." '

Maqbool's nerves had not quite recovered from the shock of the physical humiliation of the Pathan tribesmen who had chased him in the morning, when the verbal threats were hurled at him in quick succession by the supreme judge and the prosecutor. He was making up his mind to speak, but his reactions were delayed by his physical condition.

'Zaman Khan!' shouted Ahmed Shah.

'Anwar oh — Kafir!' Zaman Khan called, even as he bent over Maqbool and slapped him.

The leopard in Maqbool made him sit up after he had reeled under the blow, and his eyes and face glowed with rage. And yet, from underneath the surface layers of his mind, he felt the futility of anger against these performing puppets. He had heard of such rough justice in the old British days of the 'Quit India' movement, when Jayaprakash had been tortured in Lahore jail, and of the tortures in the concentration camps of Nazi Germany, but he had never thought that it would happen again after the world was finished — not in the backwaters of Kashmir.

'You can kill me without all this,' he spoke after all. 'Why do you want to prolong the farce?'

'Khurshid Sahib was being generous to you!' roared Ahmed Shah. 'He wanted to give you a chance. But you are an ungrateful wretch! A treacherous slave of the Hindu Maharaja and his accomplice Nehru!... Answer me, will you or will you not recant?...'

Maqbool was fascinated by the twisting mouth of the roly-poly. He watched the stiffening, small, boulder-like legs of Ahmed Shah under the fat torso. He saw the rigid stern hand of the lawyer raised in admonition. And he realised that it was no use saying anything in answer to this dummy, all wood and rag. He just stared like an idiot at the automation.

'Answer me,' shrieked Ahmed Shah, frustrated.

'What do you want to know?' Maqbool said, afraid that a gesture from the prosecutor to Zaman Khan, and the watchdogs with their rifles behind him, would assault him again. Somehow, the prolonged physical humiliations seemed worse to him than the direct blow of death, because of his inability to answer back.

Encouraged by the prisoner's response, Ahmed Shah began to hurl his questions on him:

'You went to Srinagar some days ago and came back to conduct sabotage against the liberation army of our Muslim brethren in Baramula? Give me the names of your collaborators in Srinagar and Baramula.'

The prisoner could not help grinning stupidly at Ahmed Shah's histrionic manner.

'This is no laughing matter! Answer me. What have you been doing since yesterday when you returned? Whom have you been seeing? Give me full details.'

Maqbool started at the prosecutor with a set and impassive face.

Ahmed Shah outstared him and shouted: 'How many people have you contacted since last night?'

Maqbool looked from face to face and then withdrew his eyes, because the whole court seemed like a shaken kaleidoscope before his dizzy brain.

'If you will not answer, Zaman Khan will make you disgorge the facts in his own way!' threatened Khurshid Anwar. 'If you value your life, be a good man, an honest Muslim, and answer!...'

'You are pro-Bharat still, are you not?' shouted Ahmed Shah.

'So were you once!' answered Maqbool as though speaking aloud to himself.

'But I have repudiated the traitors who have sold Kashmir to the Maharaja and to Nehru! I spit in the faces of all your leaders! I shall try them for their crimes against the people of Kashmir as soon as our armies enter Srinagar!... And you need not expect any mercy from me, because you were once known to me!... I could have saved your life if you had recanted. But you dare to insult me!...'

'Never mind,' said Khurshid Anwar, knowing that his lackey was reacting stupidly. 'Don't let us waste time. It will soon be time for the evening prayers... Proceed...' And he looked at the reddening western sky, where the sun was going down.

'You are pro-Nehru! And your leaders in Srinagar are pro-Bharat! All of you have united and called in the Indian army to desecrate the sacred soil of Muslim Kashmir, whose people want to unite with their brethren in Pakistan. And you and your friends are helping the Indian army. Admit it? — That you are a traitor?'

Maqbool's eyes had also followed Khurshid Anwar's to the western sky. What was more, he felt that he heard a distant rumbling on the horizon. And his attention was distracted, so that he heard but did not listen to Ahmed Shah's fateful indictment. His prejudice against the lawyer made him unresponsive to the mechanical intensity of the prosecutor's voice. He felt remote.

'Come to your senses! Raper of your sister,' shouted Khurshid Anwar. 'Do you not value your life?'

'I value my sister's honour more than my life!' Maqbool answered. 'So please do not abuse me like that.'

'Insolent swine!' shouted Ahmed Shah. 'You are persisting in your treachery and don't realise that a word from Mr. Khurshid Anwar — and Zaman Khan will finish you off!... Recant your treacherous stand or I shall have no option but to ask the court to pronounce judgement on you!...'

The enormity of the prosecutor's abuse suffocated him. He inhaled a deep breath, swallowed some saliva, drank his anger and remained silent.

'Speak and ask forgiveness from Khurshid Sahib!' Ahmed Shah roared.

Maqbool believed in the spacious immensity of his own choice and, though realising that there was no way of communicating a point of view which was the opposite of his judges, he nevertheless ought to tell them of his heart's felt truth.

'Truth has no voice,' he began by chewing the words in the bitter froth in his mouth to himself, so that his lips did not open and no voice could be heard. 'Only lies flourish for a while... I have no face. I have no speech. I cannot move you... This land, which gave birth to me, this land which is like a poem to me — how shall I explain my love for it to you? From out of its valleys there has risen for centuries the anguish of torture... And we were trying to emerge from the oppression to liberate our mother, because we know her each aching caress... And you have come and fouled her and wounded her! How could any of us stand by and not protest against your cruelty... All invaders behave like that. And I can understand and forgive the mercenaries. But I cannot forgive your treachery — Ahmed Shah. Do you not feel the human response of pity for the weak?'

Ahmed Shah rushed up towards him after contemplating his tight-mouthed presence for a prolonged moment, kicked him furiously, so that Maqbool fell back again.

'I demand immediate death for him. He is a self-confessed rebel! And he is unrepentant!'

'The thief accusing the sheriff!' Khurshid Anwar mumbled with a half guilty tone in his voice, because he had, in spite of himself, been moved by Maqbool's silence. Then he assumed the theatrical manner of the judge and said: 'If a prisoner cannot defend himself, then there is only one thing for it — '

He got up with a certain deliberation which showed that he felt unequal to the task of pronouncing the sentence.

'Zaman Khan, put him up there and shoot him!' said Ahmed Shah rushing towards the tall warder. 'What do you say, Khurshid Sahib? You have to give the final words!...'

Khurshid Anwar nodded, but said: 'I must ask the sanction of the higher authorities before carrying on the sentence... Zaman Khan, keep him in custody for the night in the same cell...'

Zaman Khan leant over and tapped Maqbool on the shoulders, asking him to get up.

Maqbool obeyed the behest and stood vacuously, unable to think or feel, though his heart had begun to throb again out of the instinctive love of dear life. The sense of hearing himself, a puppet among the puppet shapes of his tormentors, crept into him, with a sense of the futility of the whole thing. Automatically, he moved towards the cell of the stables where Zaman Khan led him.

~

Restored to the darkness of the cell, Maqbool was partially relieved, though, in another part of his being, he wished that they had ended his agony by executing him there and then, after the summary trial, rather than consign him to this suspense again. And yet, somewhere in a corner, there lurked the hope of a reprieve.

His nerves were worn out by the violence of the interrogation and he felt tired and lay down on the bed.

With the nightfall outside, the gloom of the room increased and, though his eyes got used to the dark, he could not see much.

He tried to sleep, but waves of delirium ran through him, making his violent heart drum against his will; and there was an ache at the back of his head and on his temples. He wanted to reach out among the flashing stars before his shut eyes for the reasons of this disturbance. But his mind seemed to have been emptied out of all content, because a numbness spread from inside him, enveloping him and making him part of the inert darkness around him. It was as if he had been suddenly paralysed and left listless and cold like a frozen jelly. And a peculiar chilliness seemed to be growing within him till he felt exhausted and half dead. The sheer physical fatigue had got the better of him.

As he felt like a carcass, he turned over on his side, hoping that the change of position would enable him to sleep. But the weight of the nullity in him became suspended over his body in a kind of hopelessness, which was due both to ennui and to the dim sense of coming disaster. He sighed and then smacked his lips and tried to shake off the morbid depression which lay inertly on his limbs.

There was the sound of distant rumbling of guns, a heavy zoom which lasted quite a few minutes.

He wondered if his oppressors had finished the trial quickly, because there was a heavy battle going on and they wanted to be on guard. Had the Indian army come and the heavy zoom emanated from their guns? Elated at this thought, he then thought it would be a miracle to expect that he would benefit from it, in this obscure cell in the stables of the tonga drivers of Baramula. No one would come looking for him here. And yet, perhaps, his parents might apprise them of what had happened, and they might come. His sister would certainly insist on their searching for him. And he felt a quiver of tenderness go through him at the prospect of being found and liberated...

The guns ceased to bark, however, and the forebodings that had possessed him earlier became so powerful and black that the spark of hope was extinguished.

There was nothing for it, but to turn upside down and descend into the pit of darkness, for perchance, sleep might come into his eyes...

~

The ghastliness of the nightmare was increased by the fact that in his half sleep Maqbool could also feel the dark walls of the cell to be eloquent. He was carrying his own head on the palm of his left hand, while he had a sword in the right. The familiar shapes of his mother and sister stood weeping among the crowd in the gallery... Exhausted, by the panic of his flight before the pursuing police, he was, however, still brandishing his sword. Before him now was a well from which emerged the alabaster effigy of a woman with bullet holes in the belly and on the lovely neck. The image fell, with a ringing, as of a hundred bells, and there was a splash, and the secret hidden forms emerged from a graveyard and brushed past him. And great lidless eyes roved widely searching into his eyes. He flew with all the power in his limbs from these ogling eyes. And, in a second, he had travelled through many spheres in the courtyard of a mosque in which crosses stood broken over the little mounds of graves. As he was wondering how crosses could have come to be fixed on the graves in a mosque, he became conscious of the presence of some raiders on the plinth of the mosque, shrieking,

'Allah ho Akbar!' and calling upon him, Maqbool, to surrender. Among them was the face of Khurshid Anwar, who was shouting in Punjabi, while Ahmed Shah appeared from behind the crowd and lifted him and fixed him against the sky, before a giant with a big white beard who looked like God. All the ambitions and his peculiar determinations seem to slither down from his body and fall away, as though as he was already dead, the pale ghost of himself — about to be put into a grave... But, before he could be exalted to the presence of the Omnipotent judge, or consigned to a grave, he felt that he was suspended in mid-air and —

Opening his eyes in the dark, dripping with sweat, he sensed the zooming of deafening artillery and machine gun fire.

He was sure that there was a battle raging in Baramula itself. He waited for the firing to stop. There was a brief lull. But the zooming of the big guns began again.

He tried to remember bits of his nightmare, but could only see the great bearded image of the Omnipotent judge.

He inhaled a deep breath. Filming into his brain, over the glistening tissues of the light in his eyes, he could see more snippets of his dream, wafting about. Waves of fear coursed through him...

For five minutes, he lay embroiled in the vapourous atmosphere of his dim apprehensions. Then he heard the door being thrust open.

He sat up in a panic.

Zaman Khan and the two sentries were on him.

He felt the tight throated protest of his dream arise towards his larynx, and his mouth opened, but no sound came out.

The soldiers lifted him and dragged him out.

He looked at them with a terrible curiosity, almost as though he was imploring them to tell him what they meant to do to him.

But he could not see their faces clearly and his gaze became fixed in a deathly stare in front of him...

~

The tall Pathan Zaman Khan walked ahead of Maqbool, while the other two warders followed behind him.

Strange and amorphous were his sensations now, bordering upon the hope that, perchance, the orders had come for him to be released, and the apprehension of the final shooting. There could be no other solution awaiting him, since they had dragged him out, in the middle of the night. His heart was pounding against his will...

He heard Zaman Khan say in a loud whisper: 'He is here, sir.'

And Maqbool saw the contours of Ahmed Shah, standing in the courtyard, mobile and seemingly agitated.

A hot anger surged up in him at this man's persistence in seeing him tortured, and he wanted to shout at him for all his falseness. But the noise of the bombardment drowned his fury, even as it made the lawyer more nervy.

'Quick, Zaman Khan!' Ahmed Shah shouted.

'Traitor!' began Ahmed Shah facing Maqbool. 'Lift your eyes high to Allah! Your end has come!...' And then, turning to Zaman Khan, he continued: 'I shall count one, two, three — at three the warders must shoot!'

Zaman Khan communicated the order to his men. And, adjusting himself to his full height, with his hands on his hips, he looked in the direction of Ahmed Shah.

Maqbool suppressed a sigh at the end of which the despairing cry 'mother' formed itself, and got swallowed up in the dryness of his throat. He stared at the deranged round face of Ahmed Shah, wondering why he had never been able to gauge the meanness, and hatred in this warped man. He closed his eyes and tried to conjure up the image of his sister in his mind, but her figure failed to arise.

Ahmed Shah shouted the dread numbers.

Zaman Khan repeated the orders.

At the utterance of three, two shots rang out.

There was only a blurr before Maqbool's eyes, then flashes of light, followed by waves of darkness. And his body collapsed in a heap — the blood shooting up as from a fountain.

~

For a moment Ahmed Shah's eyes blinked. Then he dug his feet solidly into the earth and ordered Zaman Khan:

'Lift his corpse and tie it to the pole behind him. And write the word *"Kafir"* on his shirt with his own blood. The whole population of Baramula should know that treachery is punishable only with death.'

The glint in his eyes was liquid under the red pupils. And Zaman Khan seemed mesmerised by his orders, as he began to do faithfully what he had been told.

As Ahmed Shah's inflated body moved, his shrunken soul quivered involuntarily to see the flashes of artillery fire over Baramula. He wanted to mumble a prayer from the Koran, but words would not come to his mouth. In a panic, he shouted, as though to fill his craven soul with confidence:

'Allah ho Akbar!'

~

The next day, when the Indian troops entered Baramula, they found almost half the town razed to the ground. And, as they combed the streets and houses, they entered the Mughal caravanserai and found the body of Maqbool Sherwani tied to a wooden pole in the stables, with the word *'Kafir'* written on the lapel of the shirt... The body looked almost like a scarecrow, but also like that of Yessuh Messih on the cross. As they went through his pockets for a possible diary, they found a wad of papers, which were obviously a letter he had written.

~

The letter read:

> 'My sister, Noor, we shall not see each other again... They have brought me here to the stables in the ruined caravanserai and put me in a dark room. And though, at first, the verdict was not given, their faces spoke clearly enough of their intentions. "You are a traitor. And you will be tried and shot." As they did not say these words in the beginning, I was not quite certain of my fate. But their faces were not human. And their eyes were withdrawn. And they have handled me so roughly that I felt the judgement was clear enough. So I too remained silent and did not ask my questions... What questions can one ask these murderers from Pakistan, who have attacked our country? They consider any one who defends Kashmir to be a traitor. Surprisingly, my old friend, the lawyer Ahmed Shah, who is a real traitor, both to friendship and to our country, is favoured by them. And they have declared Jehad, a holy war, to save us Muslim brethren from the embrace of the Hindus of India. To confer freedom on us by force seems the sheerest folly. Often in human life, stupidity wins and decency is on the losing side...

'I know that you have always thought of me as somewhat of a hero, Noor. Always there was a light in your big eyes which said so. But, today, I want to write and tell you, so that you can tell everyone that I have never been anything but an aspirant to poetry. All my dreams will remain unfulfilled, because I am going to face death. But here, in our country, the most splendid deeds have been done by people, not because they were great in spirit, but because they could not suffer the tyrant's yoke, and they learnt to obey their consciences. And conscience, howsoever dim, is a great force, and is the real source of poetry. For, from the obedience to one's conscience, to pity, is but a small step. And pity is poetry and poetry is pity. In our beloved Kashmir today, no one can be human without listening to his conscience, and to the orchestra of feelings without voices which is our landscape. And everyone who listens is being true to our heritage of struggle.

'When I was in Srinagar the other day and was sitting around, trying to decide what to do, whether to stay in the capital or come back to Baramula, to organise the struggle here, I asked the advice, not of a leader, but of a young Punjabi sitting next to me. He said: "No one can advise you. Because it is important in these times, that a man should consult himself. There are Pakistanis who have come to fight in Kashmir, most of them because they were promised loot, but some of them, consciously, because they want to conquer this country and make it part of their 'Pure' State. They, too, these men, are facing the danger of death. And they fight well, at the moment better than we are doing! But that is not heroism. It is just gangster pride. If you choose to go to Baramula, your deed will be heroic, because you will be facing death in the defence of your home, while they are trying to conquer other people's territory. I know what your choice will be..."

'I am writing this to you, because I could not explain to mother and father why I came back. And as you are young, and always had that light of hope in your eyes when you looked at me, I know you will understand why I made the choice I did make. And, some day, you will be able to explain this to our parents. It is better that they should know this, because I should not like to think that they thought I was just impetuous and foolhardy, and because I would not like them to indulge in vague sentimental feelings, about what might have been if I have not come back. Strange, but this is my philosophy of life — that I love people!... And I want father and mother to accept this truth than the lie which their love for me dictates...

'And now I am a little sad that I always refused mother's advice and did not agree to marry. Because in this she was right. It is foolish not to have children. Life should continue. It should prevail against death. For it is to help life to continue and prevail and flourish in Kashmir that we are suffering and dying... I would have been more contented in facing the future, if there had been growing up, in our household, an heir to my poet's longings and aspirations. If life continues, then death, even sudden death, is as reasonable as birth, or life itself...

'You are the only person to whom I could have written these words. Because you are a young girl with dreams of your own and will soon understand what I am saying. I did not write to father because I know he will say that I exaggerate everything in my "vagabond poet's manner" and he will not understand that raising everything to the highest pitch may be romantic, but it is necessary when death has raised the value of life. And when you are married and have a child, I want you to remember this and let your offspring bear my name. I think your husband will permit this, because I am sure you will choose an enlightened man to be your companion in life... And your child will grow up and work for our lovely land, and through him or her, my spirit will be working for the new life in our country.

'There is hardly any light and I cannot write more.'

~

P.S. 'I am adding some more words to my previous words. They took me out and tried me. Ahmed Shah demanded my death on the charge that I am a proven traitor. The Pakistani officer is asking his headquarters for confirmation of this sentence. I think the dice is loaded against me on the chess board... I am glad that they have warned me about death. But there is very little doubt left now and suspense would have been more terrible than is this certainty. And, with the certainty of death before me, I can renew my faith in life. I shall love life with the last drop of my blood. And I want you to cherish this love of life, because you are young and will understand this love... I kiss you tenderly on your forehead and on each of your big black eyes.'

❑❑❑

GLOSSARY

Acha	Expression for 'well! all right' used in the Indian subcontinent.
Adab arz	Urdu word for salutation or greeting.
Allah-ho-Akbar	God is great.
Allah-Mian	Another respectful name for Allah.
Amla	Hindi for Indian Gooseberry.
Angrezi	English language, and/or anything associated with England.
Angrezi Sarkar	Reference here is to British Government.
Babuji	A respectful title or form of address for a man, especially an educated one.
Bachu	A friendly expression for the person being addressed.
Badshah	King.
Bahin chod Angrez log	Sister fucker. In the story it is used as an obscenity to denounce the British.
Bazaar	A market place.
Bhut/Bhoot	Literally, demon, ghost or an evil spirit.
Churel	Witch or a hag.
Dagdar	Distortion of English word 'Doctor'.
Dur, Dur	To shoo away.
Gentermana	North Indian rural distortion of the word 'Gentleman'.
Gulley	An alley.
Hai-hai	Alas! Alas!
Han	Yes.
Harami	Bastard.
Hun	A grunt indicating assent.
Izzat	Honour, reputation.

Jinns	Evil spirit capable of appearing in human and animal forms and possess humans.
Kafir	Non-believer.
Kikar	A small tree found mainly in dry regions of the Indian sub-continent also called Babool.
Lalla	A respectful designation especially for a trader or businessman. Also spelt as 'Lala'.
Lat Sahib	Hindi/Urdu distortion of the English word 'Lord'.
Mullah	A Muslim learned in Islamic theology and sacred law.
Munshi	A North Indian expression for a clerk usually the one who writes books of accounts.
Ohe	Hey you.
Parathas	A flat, thick piece of unleavened bread fried on a griddle.
Phuphi mai	Paternal aunt (father's sister).
Pice	The smallest unit of Indian currency till the mid-20th century. Pice was a quarter of an anna in value.
Pir	A Muslim saint or a holy man.
Purdah	The practice among women in certain Muslim societies of dressing in all enveloping clothes, in order to stay out of sight of men or strangers.
Railgari	Train
Raj	Rule
Rajah	King
Sahib	A polite form of address for an educated, cultured man.
Salam alaikum	Arabic language greeting in Muslim cultures, meaning 'Peace be upon you.'
Sale	Literally, wife's brother. Also an abuse implying that the speaker has slept with the sister of one addressed. Also spelt as 'saale'.
Sajdah	An Arabic word meaning prostration to God in the direction of Kabba at Mecca.
Sari	A garment consisting of a length of cotton or silk elaborately draped around the body, traditionally worn by women from the Indian sub-continent.

Sarkar	Literally, the government. It also refers to a person in a position of authority, especially one who owns land worked by tenant farmers.
Shalwar/Salwar	A pair of light, loose pleated trousers tapering to a close fit around the ankles, worn by men/women mostly in North India and Pakistan.
Shaitan	Devil.
Suras	A chapter or section of the Koran.
Tehmet	An unstitched length of cloth usually worn knotted at the waist by men in the Indian sub-continent. Also spelt as 'tehmad'.
Tonga-wallah	'Wallah' translated literally means 'man' and the prefix tonga (horse carriage) indicates occupation. Tonga-wallah would roughly translate as tonga-man or tonga-driver.
Topee	A hat or a cap.
Vilayat	England
Wa alaykum as-Salam	Response to *Salam alaikum* (peace be upon you) meaning 'And on you be peace!'
Wuzu	The act of cleaning oneself before namaaz.